Margaret and Erika

Two Fourteen-Year-Old Girls Battle Spies and
Murderers In the Richest Town in America

Also by R. L. Rhyse

Margaret of Greenwich
Book One In
The Margaret of Greenwich™ Series

R. L. Rhyse

Margaret and Erika

Two Fourteen-Year-Old Girls Battle Spies and
Murderers in the Richest Town in America

Book Two In
The Margaret of Greenwich™ Series

Wyston Books, Inc.

Margaret and Erika

Wyston Books, Inc.
www.wystonbooks.com

This is a work of fiction. All names, characters, places and incidents are the product of the author's imagination or used fictitiously. Any resemblance to actual events, locations or persons, living or dead, is entirely coincidental.

R. L. Rhyse
Margaret and Erika: a novel
1. Margaret of Greenwich (Fictitious character)
2. Teenage Girls Fiction
Library of Congress Control Number: 2011938051
ISBN 978-0-9832326-5-0
eISBN 978-0-9832326-6-7
Cover Photograph by Pando Hall/Photographers Choice RF/Licensed from Getty Images
BISAC: JUV 028000 (Mysteries & Detective Stories)
JUV026000 (Love & Romance)
JUV058000 (Paranormal)

I had become an avenger of blood,
to save the honor of society.
–Margaret

To react against fear is a good moral habit.
–Margaret

Margaret and Erika

Chapter 1

Though such stories are on Google News almost every month, that a fourteen-year-old could actually be raped and murdered had never seemed possible to me. Girls our age look too alive to die, though sex is never far from their minds as it was with us that day.

I had just turned fourteen which, I felt, was very different from earlier birthdays. Thirteen is the first year of being a "teen," getting your period and all that, while fourteen is, for most girls, well into it. Harriet, one of my two best friends agreed, though in not so many words.

"After your period and first date there's nothing new."

"You had your first date when you were five," I replied.

"That wasn't a date. I was playing doctor."

"You probably turned him off sex for life."

"He was three months older than me."

"But girls grow up faster," I replied, ending this topic of discussion.

It was another hot summer afternoon in Greenwich which we had spent moping around. Riding our bikes from my house to the main street, Greenwich

Avenue, and then walking the half mile of its length several times.

We went from the movie theater at the Metro North railroad station past the stores and small parks to the top of Greenwich Avenue. Soon we would be going to the library yet again.

This was how we spent our summer days since my family became poor and Hillary's mother, because of her lousy grades, had stopped her allowance. Now neither of us could afford to take the town ferry to one of the two local beaches.

So we did everything that was free. This wasn't much for Greenwich is the richest town in America, a place where few people bother to check the price before buying anything.

But the large Apple store was free and we went there every day to check our Facebook pages on their iPads. While hanging around, we always tried to look like the other local teenagers, almost all of whom had their own credit card with no buying limit. We pretended to be seriously considering buying one or more Macs, for ourselves or as a present for a relative.

You can only put on this act for so long. A customer who comes into a store every day and never buys anything quickly becomes labeled for what they are: a freeloader. But the staff was always polite and I told myself that a store which looks busy is better than an empty one and so we *were* valued by them. Still, even I didn't believe this.

I stared at the customers and sighed. Life in Greenwich, or anywhere else, wasn't easy for a teenager whose family had to survive on food stamps, the Mormon food bank, and their father's small Social Security Disability payments.

I signed-off from my Facebook page and looked over at Hillary. She stood beside me and was typing furiously.

"I just *loved* your economic plan. It was so democratic!" her line read.

I turned away, feeling bored. Hillary was sending another of her daily E-mails to former President Clinton. He lived in Chappaqua, New York, fifteen miles and a short bike ride away.

Unlike her past crushes this one had lasted though she had to share it with many, far older women across America. Teenagers usually look in their high school for a boyfriend but Hillary liked challenges. Or maybe, having been brought up by a single mother, she was seeking the father she never had, a super-father who had been the father of our country. And he *was* a father but just not hers.

"He is *so* handsome even with his white hair. We could make beautiful babies. What does his wife have that I don't?"

Maybe common sense, I thought but didn't say it. I just listened, being used to Hillary's ways and already knowing that sometimes what a friend wants is only to be listened to.

"Am I ugly?" she persisted.

"You must be kidding," I said, now being honest.

Hillary's hair was in the new balayage style, which was the current sun-kissed rage in Greenwich and really complimented her. I did this by painting the hair strands around her face, making them a little lighter than the base color. Her face shone with youth and innocence.

My Hillary was both gorgeous and smart. She had achieved the Honor Roll every year in our highly competitive Greenwich school until discovering sex. Now that was the only subject she excelled in, probably because she only read books about sex and childbirth.

Breast-feeding and Caesarean birth were her current major interests. Plus former President Clinton's long autobiography. All of which couldn't hurt her, I thought, being a big reader myself. If more teenagers spent more time reading they'd get better jobs and there would be greater progress in the world.

Our next routine stop, after leaving the Apple store, was to a small park just up Greenwich Avenue. There, we sat and gossiped until walking very slowly to the Greenwich library so that it took us ten minutes.

There seemed too many hours to go until I could sleep and have my dreams of love and adventure.

Dreams of sex too though I intended to have sex only after marriage, even if I already knew that marriage didn't solve everything. I also had a nightmare of being stabbed, which almost happened to me five months before.

The only change in my summer routine was on Sundays when I joined my family for the three hour service at our Mormon church. Afterward, there was the usual family dinner: vegetarian for me and meat loaf for the others. Then my sisters, nine-year-old Melanie and seventeen-year-old Melody, would disappear into their rooms, I would go to mine, my father would go to his home office, and my mother would clean. It relaxed her.

I was afraid that all of my teenage life would drag on like this. Having a job would make things better but those that were available had long since been filled by older teenagers, almost all of whom didn't need the money but wanted the experience of working. And most businesses wouldn't hire anyone under sixteen, some not even under eighteen.

Hillary had her Bill to fantasize about and I had my Randy. But because no real life lover could compete with a fantasy one, my moping continued. Or maybe it is that I'm depressed, I thought. That the events during my thirteenth year had taken too much out of me.

During those twelve months Greenwich had witnessed two murders, my near murder, and a financial and sex scandal which was largely hushed up. Like I always say, rich people know how to keep things quiet.

But good things happened that year too. Randy, who was now also fourteen, had finally realized that he loved me; and I made a new and maybe lifelong friend: Erika, the only child of Greenwich's most eligible widower, who was also a billionaire.

And of greatest importance, my father's Lyme disease had gotten no worse; and Mother Marie, the spiritual guide who had introduced me to my husband, the Orisha God Babaluaiye, would soon celebrate her eighty-first birthday and remained in excellent health. There was much which I had to be thankful for.

Still, I felt bored, as do many children who lack

the activities and structure which school provides in their life. I waited for something to happen. For Randy to again tell me again, for just the third time, that he loves me? For a friend needing help?

No, I told myself firmly, definitely not. One such crisis in a person's life is enough though even I knew that to experience only one crisis in a lifetime is indeed a blessing.

I sat outside and watched the sunset. Then I watched a movie with my older sister.

Melody is graduating high school the next year. She then hopes to attend a state college and to study film. I say "hopes" because college is expensive, my family is poor, and she might have to stay home to work and help keep us above water even if my father refuses to consider this.

He insists that all of his daughters will go to college, that he's already feeling better, and that many people get over Lyme disease and return to work.

To which I thought but didn't say: *maybe.* Even I knew that many of them don't, and that the government doesn't hand over Social Security Disability benefits lightly. A person must be unable to do any full-time work for at least one year, as my father had been unable to do for the past five years. Though, being a lawyer, he did handle occasional cases. Simple ones requiring only that he complete a form or send a letter, which my mother would type for him. But having to meet deadlines and to be in court regularly, as working lawyers must do, was still far too much for him. Our family knew that and so did the government.

The many movies which my sister checked out from the library reflected her career interest and dream. That she would teach film and write books about them, rather than wind up as a waitress at a local restaurant, maybe The Ginger Man or Mediterraneo.

Chapter 2

"She's never found peace since she left his arms, and never will again till she's as he is now," Erika said.

"Who are you talking about?" I asked.

I was totally confused. Erika lay on the chaise lounge as I sat on the floor, doing her nails with O.P.I.'s coral-pink shade.

Not that she couldn't afford to have them done at one of Greenwich's pricey salons but her father, the local billionaire with a fortune which national newspapers had estimated as four billion dollars plus, didn't believe in spoiling his daughter. So her allowance consisted only of what she received after washing one of their six cars, or after filing his papers and straightening his home office following a business meeting.

Erika sighed in response to my question. Finally she murmured, "Sue."

I was still baffled. "Sue who?"

Erika turned from the E-book on her iPad. "Sue, Jude's lover in Thomas Hardy's *Jude the Obscure*," she explained.

"Oh." How any teenager could enjoy reading Hardy's novels escaped me. One after another—*Far from the Madding Crowd, The Return of the Native, The Mayor of Casterbridge, Tess of the d'Urbervilles,* and *Jude the Obscure*—I and all the other students in my English class had suffered along with Hardy's characters. Our teacher, Mrs. Carrobin, loved this author as had every English teacher in Greenwich for the past hundred years though the students hated his books. All except Erika it now seemed. One could never account for taste, even in a billionaire's daughter.

"His short, miserable life," Erika continued. "The deaths of his children, the opposite expectations of the two women he loved. All was gloomy."

Now I listened seriously to Erika. She was depressed again, going through what she called, simply, "my mood." This would happen to her anytime, even in the midst of a party when everyone was laughing, as she had been just the moment before. Suddenly her beautiful face would tighten and her eyes become empty. Like she saw her future and didn't like it, or that a memory from her past had popped up and she liked it even less.

Being maybe her only real friend though she had hundreds of acquaintances, I had tried to understand her. But, like my lawyer-father said, don't conclude anything until you have the facts. And these she rarely volunteered, except for the colorful stories she told.

The celebrities she met with her father. The rides on their private helicopter, on which I sometimes tagged along. Even the security room on each floor of their mansion which held loaded guns. She grinned as she described it but her eyes weren't smiling.

Some topics, even movies which contained their fictional scenes, were off limits: anything including a rape or suicide or murder.

Her sensitivity about death I could understand. Her mother had died when she was a child and I saw the longing in her eyes when she viewed *both* my parents. Though I was often annoyed by my too nervous mother, having her was far better than having no mother at all.

But why did the topic of rape so disturb her, I wondered, not that this was a topic favored by any girl, or boy for that matter. Had she been raped and this become her never-to-be-spoken-of memory? But she was still thirteen: her fourteenth birthday wouldn't arrive for two months yet. Rape rarely happened to one so young.

Still, this wasn't a question which I could ask her. "Were you ever raped?" or "Why does seeing a movie about rape so bother you?" I expected that when she was ready she would tell me. What I didn't expect was that her explanation would come so soon.

Though Hillary and Erika were my two best friends, the three of us rarely got together. Each had very different personalities so though they smiled upon meeting, they tended to grate on one another.

Hillary was pretty and bright and flirty and impulsive. Erika was moody and brilliant and so beautiful that strangers found it hard to believe how intelligent she was. As if beauty and brains couldn't go together.

So an unspoken agreement arose between us: Mondays, Wednesdays, and Fridays I saw Hillary; and Tuesdays, Thursdays, and Saturdays I spent with Erika. On Sunday morning my family went to church and all those afternoons were spent with the family. It had been this way since I could remember.

While the days and location differed, what I did with Hillary and Erika was pretty similar. We gossiped and rode our bikes and then talked some more. Despite, maybe because of, her father's wealth, Erika was sensitive to my family's poverty so the things which I did with her were also free, like with Hillary. And since the summer was a hot one and her home was frigidly air-conditioned, we tended to hang out there.

My home was also air-conditioned but we couldn't

afford to run the unit. For that same reason we no longer had a cable connection for our TVs or an Internet connection for our aging computers.

Erika's father set one rule over her life: that she must always be accompanied by a bodyguard. Apart from this, he trusted her to behave sensibly and she always did. "The wealthy have their worries too," she once remarked, and this situation required no explanation. That Erika was a tempting kidnap victim was obvious to everyone.

But even with the amusements available in her home—a seventy-two inch, 3D LCD TV with hundreds of DVDs; a pool table; a forty foot wide, one hundred and sixty-four foot swimming pool; small battery operated cars—we soon got bored.

I mentioned this in a phone call to my Aunt Lena, who owned and ran Rillston Hospital, the local private mental hospital. It was her suggestion which rescued us.

"We need a volunteer."

"Anything," I said, feeling desperate. The three of us had run out of gossip.

"Listen first before you decide," she advised. "Our newest patient is just your age, fourteen, and she needs friends. She just sits and mopes."

"Like us," I said. I already sympathized with this girl.

Aunt Lena continued. "For obvious reasons I can't tell you anything about her but her doctor suggested that getting together with girls her age would be helpful. Our next older patient is nineteen and they have little in common. I can't pay you because of state regulations but you would be doing a very good deed. "

"Could Erika come with me?" I asked. Aunt Lena had met her at my birthday party, and later discussed medical business opportunities with her father.

"That would be even better. Two would make your meeting seem more natural, like a girl's day out even if she can't leave the hospital. You could walk on the grounds or use the swimming pool or rec room or hang out in the cafeteria. And remember, all of our food is free. You could have lunch or whatever snacks you like."

"Erika's bodyguard would have to come too."

"Fine, so long as he stays in the background and keeps his gun hidden."

"He's tactful about that."

As I expected, Erika jumped at this opportunity to escape boredom into a worthwhile activity. Moreover, being a volunteer was practically her middle name. And she liked Rillston Hospital: the psychologist who was treating her had his office there.

Her bodyguard drove us to Rillston Hospital in one of the family's two armored Mercedes SUVs.

I wondered how necessary this was but the car was an impressive one. Though looking ordinary, in addition to its bullet-proof body the car had its own air supply to protect against poison gas or tear gas attack.

Specially built compartments under the front and rear seats held two short barreled sub-machine guns with extra ammunition. That impressed me. Almost every teenage boy I knew would kill to be able to hold them, to make a small pun. Except, of course, for my boyfriend, Randy, who was into math and science,

But we didn't play with the guns even though the chief of her family's bodyguard staff, Ivan, a retired bachelor detective who Erika regarded as an uncle and was treated like a member of her family, had been taking her to a shooting range since the death of her mother. Erika proved to be a talented pupil.

Beauty and brilliance and killing skills in this thirteen year old girl with the kindest heart of anyone I knew. It was a strange combination even in this often puzzling world.

We arrived at Rillston Hospital a little after eleven. Dr. Bradley, the patient's psychologist, met us in the cafeteria and told us a little about her.

"Maureen has been here since Thursday so this is her third day. She has her own room as do all of our patients, and can walk freely about the grounds but not leave the hospital though it is wide open. As you probably noticed, there are no guards and the gate is always kept open."

As he said this he glanced at Erika's bodyguard who sat beside her. Sometimes Ivan listened closely but more often he scanned the room for potential threats.

I watched them and had an odd thought: I knew that Ivan would protect Erika with his life for that was what he was being paid to do. But if danger arose, would he protect me too? And might this again become necessary as it had been just a few months before, in wealthy, apparently peaceful Greenwich,

I wondered why this odd thought stayed glued in my mind: how many people got hit by lightning twice?

Dr Bradley continued. "We don't know much about Maureen. One might almost say that she was dropped off like the proverbial baby in a basket at a hospital's door. But with Maureen it had been by government officials who paid for a year of her treatment in advance, with a promise of more money if it was needed. 'Whatever is necessary,' they said.

"Apparently both of her parents worked for a government agency and died abroad. That's all we know, plus some family history which seems to have nothing to do with her current symptoms.

"Rillston Hospital specializes in the short-term treatment of emotional problems. In the past it treated patients for months or even years. That was in the good old days before managed health care came in, when treatment could last for as long as was needed. Now, many hospitals have to discharge patients after a few days.

"Treating patients briefly is hard on a staff. As soon as the admissions paperwork is completed, it's time to begin all over again. That's why we have a big staff turnover. You might say that Maureen's treatment is a bit of an experiment for us. We're opening a unit offering long-term treatment for those who can afford it, which is an increasing number of families in Greenwich. They want their child to be healed and started on the road to a healthy adulthood. Not to live at home, unemployed and unemployable, for the rest of their life."

Dr. Bradley was certainly taking a lot of time with us, I thought. Likely it was because he knew who Erika's father was. A favorable report passed along to a billionaire could be, like they say, money in the bank.

Although his explanation appeared to be coming to an end, it seemed as if there was something else he wanted to tell us but wasn't sure how to put it. Dr. Bradley sipped his coffee for several moments as his eyes went from Erika's face to mine. Then he put down his cup.

"There's one more thing you should know about Maureen. It will explain why we are so grateful for your help. She's barely spoken since she arrived. When a patient can't speak, the doctor must talk to them. Though not to ask questions since these can cause pain for someone about whom the doctor knows little. So the doctor talks about neutral topics, movies or books, even telling stories about almost anything. Just so the patient feels comfortable, as if they were at home.

"Maureen isn't speaking to us so we are hoping that her being with other teenagers will help. In fact she repeats only one word, *room,* and we have no idea what she is trying to tell us. Maybe, being her age, she'll trust you and you can discover it. She may even open up and speak of other things. Do you have any questions?"

Now Ivan spoke that question which was central in his mind. "Is Maureen dangerous?"

Dr. Bradley seemed to roll the question in his

mouth. "Is Maureen dangerous? That's not a simple question to answer. Everyone is potentially dangerous given certain conditions. Several years ago, not far from here in New York State, a woman who was described by a relative as being 'the most responsible I knew' drove with a blood alcohol level twice the legal limit. There was evidence that she had smoked marijuana too. The woman and four young children were killed, as were three men in the SUV she drove into, along the wrong lane on the Thruway.

"But to answer your very reasonable question more directly. No, we don't regard Maureen as being dangerous. If she was, she couldn't be here since we have no locked doors or physical restraints. Patients needing these are sent to the state hospital. Any other questions?"

"How should we behave with her?" Erika asked, though I thought that I knew the answer: just like we do with our friends when they are upset. By listening and not criticizing no matter what they say, which is basically what Dr. Bradley advised us to do.

"Be a friend to her like you are with your other friends. Though your age, she'll behave as if she were younger. She'll probably trail after you and let you make the decisions."

Just like my boyfriend, Randy, acts, I thought, but didn't say it.

"You can ask her what she would like to do but she probably won't say anything. So then you suggest something and invite her along. If she wants to go, fine. If not, do your thing and return to her afterward and tell her what you did, like you would with a younger sister."

Dr. Bradley looked at his watch. "I'll take you over and introduce you. She'll be in her room."

We slowly stood up but then jolted upright upon hearing a piercing scream coming from a corner of the room. Was Dr. Bradley being serious when he denied that the patients at Rillston Hospital were dangerous?

Ivan unbuttoned his suit jacket. I focused on the outline of a pistol in his shoulder holster as he moved Erika in back of him, shielding her with his huge body.

Chapter 3

Dr. Bradley smiled reassuringly and explained. "That's nothing. It's just a young woman who is terrified by the sight of a spider even though, being in the country as we are, one can't avoid insects."

"Why is she so afraid of spiders?" Erika asked. "I could understand someone being afraid of snakes since everyone is, but a spider? There are no poisonous spiders in Connecticut and they help us by catching bugs. Spider webs are beautiful too."

"That's what most people think but that young woman isn't like most people. Her real fear has nothing to do with spiders. They just symbolize it, take the place of the fear in her mind. Worrying about the small, safe spider keeps her from facing up to her real concerns about the painful situation in her life."

What Erika then asked floored me, and probably surprised Ivan too. "Could a girl's fear of rape be symbolic too? That maybe she is really afraid of something else?"

Dr. Bradley looked at her for a moment before answering. As if he needed more information in order to give an accurate answer, information which he couldn't seek since she wasn't his patient.

Finally, he did speak. "That depends on the experiences the person had. Like Sigmund Freud, the founder of psychoanalysis once said, 'sometimes a cigar is just a cigar.' If a person was raped, the fear might linger all their life. But if it never happened, and men can be raped too, then the fear of being raped is taking the place of another worry except where rape is common, as in some prisons or war zones. Am I being clear?"

Both Erika and I nodded but as we followed Dr. Bradley from the cafeteria I wondered. Why did Erika ask? Was she or her mother raped? Certainly both had always been well protected. Or had they, I wondered, and remembered how little I really knew about Erika. But her question might also have reflected something innocent.

There was one book which we read in Honors English that the whole class did love. It was old, having been written seventy-five years ago, though not as old as the books of Thomas Hardy. But it was just as big, more than five hundred pages.

It was about a teenage girl, one which we girls could relate to though the boys liked the book too. The book was called *A Tree Grows In Brooklyn* and was written by Betty Smith.

Once I started reading this book I couldn't put it down and when I finished it I wrote about it in maybe the best essay I will ever write. The teacher, Mrs. Carrobin, thought so too and she gave me an A plus on it. She said that it was the first A plus which she ever gave and had me read it to the five English classes she taught. Despite my fear of being in front of an audience I did OK. Except for my last reading when my eyes suddenly filled with tears because I realized that my life was so much like that of the main character in the book, Francie. She was eleven when it opened.

Mrs. Carrobin might even, in her own way, have been trying to tell me that despite all of my family's troubles things could turn out OK if I fought to survive like Francie did.

My family is poor like Francie's but while she lived in a terrible apartment in a New York City tenement in nineteen hundred and eleven, we live in a nice house in Greenwich which, as I said, is the richest town in America.

She had a younger brother, Neeley (short for Cornelius) while I have a younger and older sister. Her mother worked by cleaning apartment buildings and her father, because of his drinking, could earn only a little money as a singing waiter. My father is a lawyer but he can't work because of his Lyme disease. My mother was a teacher but she couldn't find a local job and the part-time job she did get as a school secretary only lasted a few months until she was let go. The school lost a funding grant.

This left my family back where we were for the previous five years when my dad got sick: surviving on my father's Social Security disability payments; and food from the Mormon food bank, the government's Food Stamp program, and gifts from people who my father helped in his law practice. They give us fruit and vegetables from their farms.

But there are differences between me and Francie too: her grandparents were recent Irish immigrants while my ancestors had been in America for two hundred years. They live throughout the United States but mostly in Connecticut and Utah. And unlike Francie's father but like those in most Mormon families, no one in my family ever touches alcohol, or smokes or even drinks coffee.

Francie relied on her imagination and reading to escape the poverty in her family. This is another similarity between us.

Erika also read this book though she couldn't

identify with Francie as I did since for her father is rich. But there was one part of the book which did grip her, and might be why I thought of it when Erika talked about rape. It was when Francie's mother, Katie, saved Francie's life by shooting a child-rapist-murderer who attacked Francie when she was thirteen—which is just how old Erika was when she read the book.

I wondered about the possible connection between them and then put it out of my mind. If I spent time thinking about every upsetting scene in a book or movie I would never get anything done. Particularly with all the torture movies now being made for teenagers but which I refuse to watch.

In any case, our job now was to become friends with Maureen. That was what Dr. Bradley and my Aunt Lena were relying on us for.

While we walked to Maureen's room, Dr. Bradley described Rillston Hospital.

"The main setting is made up of three interconnecting one story buildings shaped like a U within which we are now at the base. On one side are the doctors' offices and business offices; the other side contains individual rooms for the patients. At the base of the U, where we just were, are the cafeteria and recreation rooms. The swimming pool is in a separate building.

"There is also a small building made up of motel-like units. There, family visitors can stay while they are visiting patients. We plan to have the long-term patients spend their nights there during the last weeks before their discharge. This is to give them the experience of being 'outside' once again.

"During the day, patients attend psychotherapy groups, have their own individual therapy, or do pretty much whatever they enjoy doing. We provide structure but are not rigid about it. The hospital's philosophy, one which your aunt wrote and has won it awards, is to make the hospital as similar to a normal home as possible.

"So each patient's room is different and if a patient doesn't like how it's decorated, we'll move her to another room if one is available. Otherwise we'll see if another patient will change rooms with her."

"This sure isn't like school," I remarked, and everyone smiled.

Speaking more softly than he had before, Dr. Bradley said, "There's one more thing you should know about Maureen so if she refers to it you won't think that she's crazy in the sense of what most people consider craziness. When Maureen arrived here she had a complete medical examination. What we found surprised us: she's had a baby."

Erika and I stared at each other, not knowing what to say. Ivan's face remained blank, likely because he probably had heard just about everything before retiring as a detective.

Maureen wasn't in her room. She sat in a window alcove. She held a book in her lap but it was obvious that she hadn't been reading since the book was upside down. It was a well-worn book and probably came from the hospital's library. An old Nancy Drew novel, the adventures of a teenage detective who had thrilled generations of girl readers since they were first published in the nineteen-thirties. Though now dated, they are widely approved of by Mormon families for their healthy morals. I read them.

Maureen turned from the window as we approached but she didn't say anything. She was dressed in a striped green and white T-shirt and faded jeans. She should have worn a bra but wasn't. Maybe in another hospital they would have insisted on this, I thought. Made it a part of her prescribed treatment along with the medication. Aunt Lena had told me that medication was little used at Rillston Hospital.

The clothes which Maureen wore were on about

the same level as those I got at the Salvation Army store in Port Chester. But this didn't matter for she would have looked stunning in a sack.

Erika was beautiful in a wholesome old-fashioned way: the blue eyed/blond haired goddess of nineteen fifties pinup calendars. But Maureen's beauty was something different and, despite her obviously Irish name, she was definitely not conventionally Irish.

Her high cheekbones reflected a Slavic or Nordic parentage while her eyes were definitely Oriental. She was a Eurasian mixture of Europe and the Orient. Ivan seemed to recognize her and I wondered if he had known someone like her.

Dr. Bradley nodded towards us. "This is Erika and Margaret. They live in Greenwich and Margaret's aunt is my boss so please be nice to them. They'll be spending every other day keeping you company but you'll be the boss and decide what to do. Or you can follow their lead, hang out with them awhile and then go off on your own and meet up with them later. It's up to you. Erika has a bodyguard to protect her. His name is Mr. Ivan and he won't interfere with your activities. You also can't date him." Dr. Bradley said this with a small smile which all of us except Maureen joined and that was it. Erika and I were on our own.

Not knowing what to do, but feeling that Dr. Bradley knew best, we followed his advice and began chatting about teen stuff. We didn't pressure Maureen to join us but tried to appear open to it.

"What's Randy doing over the summer?" Erika asked me.

"Randy is my boyfriend," I explained to Maureen. "He's volunteering at the local hospital. He hates it but his father is pressuring him to be a doctor though his volunteer work has nothing medical about it. He files papers and works the cash register in the gift shop. When he runs out of work he reads, as usual." Randy was a big reader like me.

"That seems a waste for such a smart guy."

"It is," I replied. "But the trouble he got into scared his parents so now their biggest interest is keeping him on the 'straight and narrow' as they put it."

"Meaning they want to keep him away from us," Erika said with a smile, which I joined. Randy's troubles had come from his agreement to help us do a good deed for a friend.

What now, I thought. Standing and chatting amongst ourselves while Maureen sat and held a book upside down didn't seem helpful, or courteous.

I felt that we should do something, but what?

It was Erika who saved us. "I'm hungry. Let's go to the cafeteria." Then she put out her hand. After several moments, just when it seemed that her hand would remain untaken, Maureen hesitantly grasped it. I took Maureen's other hand and we walked in silence to the cafeteria.

Though she was older than both of us, and had adult experiences we had not, she behaved like a child and looked to us for guidance. I felt like I was walking with my nine year old sister.

I also felt talked out and Erika seemed that way too.

The noise in the cafeteria made up for our silence and once we got there there Maureen became more animated, no longer seeming like a frozen porcelain doll.

The cafeteria was a familiar setting for her and doing the usual, getting on line with others and making her food selection, seemed to pull her out of herself though she still didn't speak. Not even her mysterious word, "room."

My thoughts drifted to having sex and becoming pregnant at thirteen (for Maureen was now fourteen). What must it have been like for her? The pain of the first sex (I had heard that it could hurt) and the far greater pain of childbirth, which my mother's friends whispered about (Mormons usually have much bigger families than mine). But these women were adults. What must pregnancy have been like for a child? Could I have endured it? No wonder Maureen could not, or did not want, to speak.

I wondered how she would get food in the cafeteria without speaking but this turned out not to be a problem. The staff knew her and met her needs. For the food which required a choice she simply pointed at it, and since all of the food was free there was no cashier to have to deal with.

It was lunch time and Maureen chose a normal lunch, one like ours. Ordinarily, had there been a charge, I would have chosen the cheapest sandwich or a piece of fruit and a container of milk. But since all of the meals here were free, I chose the grilled salmon with spinach and carrots, rice pudding, and milk. Erika had the baked chicken with a baked potato and peas and milk too.

Since Maureen seemed depressed I would have expected her to eat little. But she had both the salmon and chicken, a baked potato, spinach, apple pie with ice cream, and milk.

All that food caused me to wonder whether the

"room" she continually referred to might not have been some kind of prison. Or maybe, having been pregnant, her body was just re-stocking itself.

Pregnant! What had become of her baby, I wondered. Did it die prematurely? Was it placed for adoption, or being cared for by a foster parent or at the local hospital? All of these were questions without answers since Maureen wasn't speaking and, if Dr. Bradley knew, he hadn't been willing to tell us. So while we ate, I continued wondering.

Chapter 4

Erika and I ate slowly, like we were used to having three meals a day. But Maureen shoveled the food down her mouth as if she hadn't eaten in days. Or been where her meals had been tiny or not regular, I thought. Like if she had been a prisoner, and maybe in the "room" she referred to.

Maureen finished eating well before we did. Then she just sat there, as if she were waiting for us to suggest something. This made me and probably Erika feel uncomfortable. So I said that I'd like to get more food and Erika acted as if this was the best idea which she heard all summer. Hand-in-hand the three of us returned to the food aisle, which by now had become crowded while we were eating.

Both the patients and the staff ate in the same dining room and several people greeted and waved to Maureen. But she didn't respond even if she was looking directly at them and they didn't seem upset. This was, after all, a mental hospital where peculiar behavior was to be expected.

Maureen chose more fish and chicken and soup and an "everything" bagel. Erika chose cheesecake and iced tea; I took a whole-wheat bagel and apple juice. We walked slowly back to our table.

Dr. Bradley passed us and smiled but didn't say anything. I guess that he didn't want to interfere with our socializing.

Once back at our table, Erika and I began eating very slowly and talking. We were trying desperately to find some topic which Maureen would respond to.

Erika spoke of an old TV series which she had seen on Netflix. It was called *Philly* and described the life of a newly divorced lawyer, her son who was about nine, her ex-husband who was the district attorney, and other lawyers and their clients.

One story from the series which Erika told us was about a big-time mobster who hires the lawyer to get his daughter, a drug addict, out of jail. The lawyer wasn't certain that she wanted to work for him but did for the sake of his daughter. Later, the lawyer took up his offer of help when another gangster threatened her client who had robbed his house.

Erika said that there were two or three ongoing stories in each episode, along with several love relationships which usually didn't go well. The lawyers were more successful in their practices than with their lives. Very realistic, I thought.

I found Erika's story interesting but Maureen's face remained blank. She kept staring out the window at the hospital grounds though I didn't think that she actually saw any of it.

She was too much into herself, like when she held the book she was supposedly reading upside down.

But Erika's next story from *Philly* caused a reaction in both her and Maureen.

This story was about a young woman who was held prisoner, repeatedly raped, and horribly tortured by a serial rapist. He cut her body many times with a knife and made tears in her vagina and butt-hole with a bottle.

When he is captured after raping another woman, the first victim attends his trial and, during a court recess, she tells him that she was his first victim and she wanted him to know that she survived. The rapist was out on bail and said that he would pay her another visit. The woman then shot him dead with a pistol which she began carrying for protection after her rape six years before.

The woman is arrested and tried for murder and both her attorney and the state's attorney provide good arguments.

Because the topic of rape had always seemed to

particularly trouble Erika, I wondered why she told this story. Telling it then definitely upset her for her speech became increasingly rapid and her eyes began looking feverish.

But I never did learn what happened to the woman in court because at the moment when Erika was about to tell us, Maureen let out a deafening scream which pierced the noise of the crowded cafeteria.

Ivan, who had been sitting and drinking coffee at a neighboring table, immediately unbuttoned his jacket. I wondered if he carried a taser in addition to a pistol for even if Maureen became violent, I couldn't believe that he would shoot her with a gun. But neither of these actions became necessary for very quickly both she and Erika began crying, and Ivan relaxed.

What a strange place a mental hospital must be to work at, I thought. Though the scream had shocked me, it didn't seem to bother the other diners. After a pause, their conversations resumed without more than the briefest glance at our table. Working there had made them used to crazy behavior, I thought. It might have been affecting me too. Though I had been there for only a few hours. I hadn't become upset by Maureen's scream either.

I felt puzzled why she screamed and wondered

what I should say or even if I should say anything to her. But I didn't think of her behavior as meaning that she was "crazy," which I would have just the day before.

I also found that I was starting to think like a psychologist. Or like a detective, which is maybe what a good psychologist is. Trying to figure out why people behave as they do and how to help them.

I also thought that Dr. Bradley might be pleased with our help since Maureen's scream was very different behavior from her usual silence. Maybe now she would start talking.

But what had happened to Erika? I wondered. Rather than being a hospital volunteer, would she soon become a patient?

Chapter 5

While we were eating the cafeteria had emptied. Soon just me and Erika and Maureen and Ivan were the only people left. Though the cafeteria never closed since hospitals are always open, I felt that it would be good for us to get out of there. For this was where Maureen's scream became followed by Erika crying, and I no longer felt that I understood her.

Maureen had a terrible experience so however she behaved, at least temporarily, could be considered normal. But brilliant, beautiful Erika, who everyone in Greenwich Middle School looked up to and whose extensive volunteer activities made her known even outside of the town, had begun acting crazy. Not that crying is ever crazy for anyone and, unlike boys, girls cry when they are happy too.

But Erika's crying had come out of the blue, as if Maureen's scream had triggered a very disturbing thought in Erika which caused her to let loose.

Then I remembered a conversation from our English class. Our teacher, Mrs. Carrobin, was speaking about Jane Austin. Not the quiet, retiring image that most believe her to be but how Jane Austin really was.

Having an aunt who was jailed for theft, a French relative who was guillotined (that means getting your head chopped off), and an acquaintance who liked to torture people and was into dead bodies. Austin was a very different woman than her brother, Henry, who wrote her biography, wanted people to think of her as being.

Then Erika said something strange. It actually scared me. She said that "what was most frightening was the unknown, being unable to understand the monster in front of you." Who was Erika referring to? Could it be that she was speaking about herself looking into a mirror?

In the moment following Maureen's scream, had Erika's thinking created that monster and caused her tears.

What could we then do? We might watch TV in the recreation room but there would be other patients there and I didn't feel that Erika or I could take seeing more crazy behavior at that moment. Even if there wasn't any to be seen, having to worry that it might pop up at any moment would be too much.

Besides, what TV could compete with Erika's huge 3D set? And going swimming was out since neither of us had brought a bathing suit and getting Maureen into one seemed impossible.

While we sat on the lawn discussing what to do, Maureen sat quietly beside us. But it now seemed that she was listening for at times she looked at who was speaking.

Erika wondered aloud if there were any board games we might play. I thought this would be a good idea since one can play some board games without having to speak. We asked at the front desk about game supplies. There were some in the supply room for visitors who had children, with them to borrow. Monopoly and Connect Four and Hulk Operation and Chutes and Ladders.

I voted for the Chutes and Ladders game, one which even my nine year old sister felt was too young for her. It was a simple game with figures going up a ladder or down a chute depending on which space the spinner landed. Though I hadn't expected to, I did enjoy playing it, as did Erika and, to my surprise, Maureen.

She still didn't smile even when she won, but the game engaged her interest and she began murmuring sounds of enjoyment. We played the game six times before I suggested that we return to the cafeteria for another snack. Erika seconded this suggestion with a relieved look. Being a friend to a teenager who acted like an eight year old was hard work!

Ever since I learned that I have a three hundred pound aunt living in Utah, I've tended to be careful about what I eat though no one in my family is overweight. So I took just an apple. Erika, who never puts on weight no matter how much she eats, chose a banana. Maureen had practically another full meal: grilled swordfish with corn on the cob and a side order of sliced ham. Fruit salad and milk topped off her order, and I wondered what she would look like in twenty years.

By this time it was nearly 4PM and I thought that we had spent enough time volunteering for the day. So I suggested that we walk Maureen back to her room. Erika asked if she would show us her room and she did.

The room looked like that of any teenager. There was a bookshelf, a closet, a chair and desk with a Mac on it, and a bed with a Peanuts bedspread. This seemed a little young but perhaps Dr. Bradley believed that she would feel more comfortable with it. And, as he had said, patients could exchange furnishings whenever they wished.

We made small comments about the furnishings and then left with a wave, which she didn't return. It may not be a nice thing to say but I was glad to get away from her. Like I said, talking to someone who can't or won't talk back is more than frustrating. It drives you crazy. At least babies, who also can't talk, respond in their own way. But then, I thought, Maureen did respond though not with words.

She took our hands and came with us, which must mean that she valued our company. And she had screamed when hearing Erika's TV rape story, which meant that this too must have reached her though why I didn't yet know. More psychology work or detective investigation was needed to find out but not that day. Then, I just wanted to relax, which Erika and I did.

The drive to her house was peaceful. Even with its heavy armor, the Mercedes SUV was a comfortable car. While Ivan drove, we lay in the back seat, not saying a word though I had questions.

Maureen was a stranger but Erika was my friend. In just the few months that we had been friends, we were through a lot together. She had stood by me and I vowed to stick by her no matter what she needed. Even as I wondered whether I could add anything to what her billionaire father had provided her with.

But he and the bodyguards he hired for her weren't teenagers. I doubted that she would tell him what she would share with me and maybe not even with her psychologist, who was her older than her father.

When in doubt, ask, my father-lawyer always told me. So I did ask Erika, directly like he would have done, though not in the car, for Ivan would have overheard us. I waited until we were in the kitchen where she brewed coffee for herself and opened a carton of orange juice for me.

When we first met I had told Erika that Mormons don't drink coffee or tea or alcohol. I explained that it was because of the Mormon Word of Wisdom, or law of health, which was given by God to Joseph Smith, the religion's founder, nearly two hundred years ago.

Not being religious, for Erika and her father didn't attend their Episcopalian church except for Christmas or a rare social occasion, she didn't buy my reasoning. But she also didn't argue with me and she respected my belief. Gospel or not, this rule did make sense for Mormons tend to be healthy. Not my father, of course, but his Lyme disease was caused by a bug.

Before asking my question I waited until Erika had filled her cup, which took some time. One might say that brewing coffee was almost a ritual for her, as it seems to have become for others. Orange juice is easier. You just shake the container and pour it or add water to the frozen concentrate.

Though she was just thirteen, Erika had been her father's business hostess for several years and this experience transferred into her meetings with friends. So, after getting my orange juice and brewing her coffee, she set the large kitchen table with napkins and silverware though it was just the two of us. The cookies weren't the Nabisco Mallomars which I loved, but Pepperidge Farm Milano and Geneva chocolate cookies. There were even the Verona fruit filled ones in case I might prefer these instead of following my usual passion for chocolate. Like I said, Erika was a real hostess.

She bit into a Geneva cookie, I bit into a Milano, and then I asked her.

"Why does the topic of rape so disturb you?"

Erika didn't say anything immediately. She just kept nibbling and drinking her coffee. I ate another cookie and tried the Verona this time. It was good.

Well, I told myself, I did ask and try to help her, and apparently we were still friends. Neither of us spoke while we continued eating. When we were finished we put the cup and glass and saucers into the sink and Erika placed the remaining cookies in the refrigerator. Then she finally spoke.

"Let's go upstairs. I want to show you something."

Once upstairs we walked past her room, where I

had believed she was taking me. But the room she entered was at the end of the hall and next to her father's. She unlocked the door with a key.

The room was elegantly furnished and very large, about twenty-five by thirty feet. It had more the look of an office than a bedroom. There was a desk and office chair, many bookcases some with glass doors, and a sofa with three club chairs around it. There was also a chaise lounge in the corner with a reading lamp beside it.

The furniture was all wood, in the heavily carved nineteenth century European style which is rarely seen today because of the work needed for its construction and the resulting cost. There is similar furniture in the house which I will inherit from my grandmother on my twenty-first birthday, but nothing as elaborate.

The wallpaper was pale pink and beige and the rug which covered the entire floor was thick and oriental. On one wall was a painting of an elegantly dressed woman with her hair set in the early twentieth century style. It was hard to look away from her gaze.

On the other wall was another painting. This was of a woman who was also dressed in evening wear. She held the hand of a teenage girl.

The woman was beautiful and the child was obviously her daughter. I recognized both at once: she was, apparently, as Erika looked now and would be as an adult.

"That's you," I said, "the artist's vision of how you are and will be when you grow up."

"No," Erika replied sadly. "The picture is of my older sister and my mother. Both were raped and murdered."

Chapter 6

I didn't say anything. I couldn't think of anything to say which wouldn't sound inadequate. *I feel for you. I'm sorry.* Because no words could express what she experienced, I didn't speak and felt that this was the right thing to do and I hoped that she understood.

Now it was clear why the topic of rape so greatly disturbed her, and why her father was so security conscious.

Only months before I was moments away from being murdered and, I feared, raped. But unlike Erika I didn't spend my days worrying about being raped though my experience was direct and personal. Had I then been raped and survived it would have caused me even greater trauma than was Erika's though the loss of a parent is always traumatic and the word "horrible" is too inadequate to describe the feelings. Like comparing a movie to a real life event.

Could there be more to her story, I wondered. Not merely that her sister and mother had been in the wrong place at the wrong time, as real life detectives sometimes say. If there was, I doubted that I would learn it.

My life in Greenwich, and as the daughter of a lawyer, had taught me that rich people were good at keeping their personal lives quiet, and what happened to Erika's mother and sister were the most private of matters.

But I was wrong for Erika did tell me what happened and without any questions from me. She spoke slowly and never cried, not even at her long story's frightful ending.

We were seated on the sofa and she gripped my hand as she began. "We must never speak again of what I am about to tell you. And you must never tell anyone what you have learned from me. Not if you value your life or those of everyone that you love.

"And not Randy even if you marry him someday because for him to know what I am about to tell you places his life at risk too. Now I must ask you, are you sure that you want to know?"

For a moment I wondered if Erika had gone crazy. Maybe our experience with Maureen at Rillston Hospital had tipped even the mature-for-her-age, sound minded Erika over the edge into madness. But she didn't look crazy like Maureen did, and I knew her too well to believe that she was joking. Who would possibly make up such a story, and for what purpose.

"Do you want to tell me?" I asked.

"Yes I do, but because having this information would place you in danger, the decision must be yours. I need to share the secret I'm struggling with, which has nothing to do with school or my never having had a boyfriend. A month ago, as we were leaving Lionel's wake, I offered you my friendship 'forever' and I meant it!"

I didn't answer her right away for then it wouldn't have been an honest response. I needed to think for I too had a big secret which I kept from her and, until recently, everyone. Now just Randy knew it though I felt that broadminded Aunt Lena would surely understand too.

At that moment I also realized why teenagers keep secrets from those they love and from their parents who love them the most. Because they need to explore and if they revealed all their thoughts and feelings they would be given advice which they didn't want to hear. The words "safe" and "don't," though these are the words they would someday use with their children too.

But hearing Erika's great secret might cause me to feel that I would have to share mine: how Babaluaiye, the Orisha God, had saved my life and become my husband.

Then, we would be more than friends, lifelong sisters too.

Probably because I was nervous, a thought went through my mind and I almost giggled. What silly boys sometimes say: "you show me yours and I'll show you mine." It had been a long day.

You might think that all these thoughts took a long time. But it was just moments until I said to Erika what Aunt Lena had once vowed to me. "I'll be here for you, now and forever." That was what Erika needed to hear. She began her story. It soon caused me to begin crying.

"When we started out my family was like yours before your father got sick: comfortably off, but certainly not rich. My father has a Ph.D. in math and he taught at Columbia University. That's where he met my mother. She was a doctor, a pediatrician, and worked at their medical school clinic. She loved working with kids. She could have made more money in private practice but her family had been poor and she always wanted to help families like hers.

"My parents married late in life. They were in their late thirties when my sister was born and I arrived as a surprise four years later. My father is very smart, both my parents were, and he began having problems at his job. He was just too smart and this made people jealous of him, like many are of Randy. Also, universities are very political and my dad was never good at office politics. He wasn't as deceitful as one has to be to survive. He learned how only later.

"You can probably guess what happened: a reason was created not to grant him tenure and he had to leave. This resulted in both the best and worst things in his life: he began making real money, but doing so led to the deaths of my mother and sister."

I began breathing normally again. When Erika began explaining, the shock of her first statement, that her mother and sister had been raped and murdered, seemed to stop my breathing though I knew this wasn't possible. It seemed that I had begun to identify so strongly with Erika that we had become one suffering person.

But as she continued and I listened and considered what she was saying, this feeling lessened. Now I tried to make sense of what I was learning about her family and to see how I could help her, how I could reduce the pain she was obviously still experiencing. Though I also remembered how my attempt to rescue another friend, Laurie, from her affair with her teacher had nearly led to my murder.

Wealthy, apparently peaceful Greenwich seemed to have become a hotbed of troubles.

Though Erika's house was frigidly air-conditioned, I began to feel warm and then as if my head were expanding. Just anxiety and post-nasal drip, I assured myself, you're not fainting. But I must have looked strange for Erika asked me if I was OK.

"Just overwhelmed by what you're telling me," I said. I knew that my anxiety would quickly go away as I again became involved in her story, and it did.

"You've met my dad. He's doesn't suffer fools and that's why he likes you so much." Erika smiled as she said this. It was her last smile that afternoon.

"When he lost his job teaching, he became very depressed. That's what losing your job does even if you have some money. My mom's job kept us eating and paid the new apartment's rent when we lost the low-cost one which had been provided by the university. But becoming unemployed means losing the structure in life which a person gains from their job.

"This creates all kinds of worries, some realistic and others not. Like the fear that you'll never work again and will wind up as a bum on the Bowery, even if it is now becoming an expensive place to live. And though my dad can put on an act at being social, he is really a loner. So losing his job also removed the built-in socializing he enjoyed. Our family's friends were always my mom's.

"Though he was feeling pretty down, I was too young to notice. Like most parents, mine tried to protect their children from the family's problems. But I did sense that something was wrong, even if this period in his life didn't last long.

"My dad is a brilliant guy and other people had heard how unfairly the school treated him so he soon got job offers. Some, like from the one from the National Security Agency, he turned down out of hand. He would have loved breaking codes which is what they do, but it would have meant moving to the Washington area and my mom didn't want to leave New York City where she had grown up.

"Then the Wall Street firms began calling. Quantitative investing, using formulas to decide what stocks and bonds to sell, was becoming big and enormously profitable. Working on Wall Street would mean that we could stay in New York, and also get him out of his depression. He'd gotten to a point where as soon as my mom left for work and me and my sister left for school, my dad went to Riverside Park, which was down the street from us, and played pickup chess games for money. It was more than a little comedown for a former college professor but he always won.

"My dad took the first Wall Street offer which came his way. It was a good job. It paid twice his teaching salary and had great benefits like free health insurance which covered everything including the cost of my braces. But the hours were much longer than when he taught. Then, he was home when we returned from school. At his Wall Street job he often didn't get home until nearly midnight. Some days, when things at work got really heavy, he slept on a couch in his office.

"So he wasn't completely happy on his job but, like he always says, that's why they call it work and pay to have it done. After a few years the same problem cropped up. My dad couldn't cope with co-workers who hate you because you remind them of their father or are jealous of your ability. He would try to win them over by being friendly, which is always a mistake. You have to figure out who they really are inside and give them what they need. He could never do this. I'm better at it and I think that you are too.

"So he left this job, a decision which my mother supported, and went out on his own. First consulting to individuals and then managing their money, using formulas which nobody else understood but worked well. When he set up his own hedge fund (they manage other people's money) he had to hire people but now he got along with them. My mother gave him good advice on who to hire and how to be a boss too.

"My dad is a conservative guy so he never believed that buying on credit was a good way to go. He was suspicious of what was happening to the American economy and bet against it. Which is what hedge funds do: they make bets on things. No different from what happens in Las Vegas though people on Wall Street get insulted when you say this.

"So my dad cleaned up, though he hates for me to use that term and we never speak of money. He doesn't even know how much money he has even if magazines estimate it every year. He's no longer in the business for the money. He just loves his work and likes to be right. 'Money doesn't lead to happiness,' he always says, 'striving to be excellent does.'"

Erika had been talking in a rush and, while I listened closely, my eyes must have started to glaze over. Like I said, it had been a long day.

"Can I get you juice or a sandwich?" she asked, being so like Erika. Even when troubled, she considered the comfort of others first.

I touched her hand. "No, it's OK. Please go on."

Erika continued. "Things were going well. We moved from our apartment into a townhouse on Fifth Avenue, a few blocks south of the Metropolitan Museum of Art. Our family used to hang out there all the time, and in Central Park which has a small but fabulous zoo. I went to a private school where everyone was nice. I couldn't imagine my life getting any better."

Erika suddenly stopped talking and a look of fear came over her face. I grasped both her hands in mine and she held on as if she were a small child. This, in usually strong and confident Erika!

"That's when 'Z' came into our life. I won't tell you his name. I'm even afraid to repeat it. It's best that you don't know. There's a term which Plato used, *anamnesis*. It means the loss of forgetfulness. Being unable to forget, to let painful events go. My life would be better if I could forget everything about 'Z.' He is a monster."

Chapter 7

I took a deep breath as Erika continued her story. It had begun to sound like the zombie video game adventure which Randy loved to play, where the central characters were monsters too. Was Erika's monster, 'Z,' one of these, I wondered, a creature who feasted on humans?

"What makes a prison a home?" she asked, as if out of the blue.

"I don't know."

"A prison becomes a home once you find the key, which neither me or my father have been able to find."

I must have looked puzzled.

"No, I'm not crazy, though I once nearly was. We're still looking and someday we will find it: the key to release us from our prison. That's our hope and the only thing which keeps us going. If there's a God above, we'll find it. If there's a God above we—or someone—will destroy 'Z.' But it won't be murder: it will be removing a poison from this Earth."

When my father's law clients asked how they should describe their troubles he would always tell them to "begin at the beginning." This is what I suggested to

Erika since I found the explanation which she had given me confusing.

First she tells me that her sister and mother had been raped and murdered. Yet when I first met her only a few months before she had told me that she was an only child and that her mother had died of measles while in Paris.

Was Erika certain that she wasn't crazy? She was, after all, being treated by a psychologist who charged three hundred dollars a session. But if Erika was crazy because of this then so were many teenagers in Greenwich. I had heard them discuss their "shrinks," with these appointments being penciled into their schedule between horseback riding and dance and music lessons.

So while seeing a therapist wasn't evidence of being crazy, the rest of Erika's story was more than a little weird. Like what was the actual truth about her sister and her mother for people don't usually lie about these details.

This is what I told her, but very gently since she was in a bad state. I talked to her like Aunt Lena talked to me at those times though I was becoming increasingly afraid that helping Erika might be way beyond mine or even Aunt Lena's abilities. Maybe even those of my friend, the Orisha Ifa priestess, Mother Marie, too, though I planned to consult her.

"Erika, I'm your friend and will be with you no matter what. But I am puzzled. First you tell me that you are an only child and that your mother died of measles in Europe and now you tell me this. Which is it?"

"What I'm telling you now is the real truth," Erika said. "When you hear it all, you'll understand why I spoke as I did. I was trying to erase the facts, maybe hoping that in this way they would no longer exist. But they do exist and once you learn them, then we'll be real sisters and not just casual friends.

"My father's investment advice was successful and soon he had people begging to let his company invest their money. Here, we are talking about real money, not thousands but hundreds of millions and billions of dollars. The world is awash in money needing a safe place for deposit and growth so that one million will soon become two million and more.

"'Z,' one of my father's clients, was a wealthy elderly European. No one knew where he came from originally. Some said Turkey, others said Germany, and a few believed that he was born in Albania. But he had lived for years in Paris and become a French citizen along the way. He lived with a mistress though he had a wife and children somewhere. No one seemed to know much about him except that he was very rich and committed to becoming even richer.

"My father accepted his business. He didn't know any more about him than he did about many his clients. But you don't generally question someone closely who is ready to wire hundreds of millions of dollars to you and is vouched for by politicians, which 'Z' had been. 'Money buys important friends' is another of my father's sayings.

"My father and 'Z' did business for several years and both got wealthier. 'Z' was pleased and sent presents: a jade necklace for my mother, a diamond encrusted watch for my sister, an elaborate electric horseback riding coach for me, like the ones you see in malls which take a quarter. We sent him thank you notes but never saw him since he rarely left Paris.

"My father is an honest guy. He's too much of a worrier and too conscientious to be anything else. He had begun to feel uneasy about 'Z.' Not because of their phone contacts for on the phone 'Z' had the ability to make everything sound wonderful. But my dad heard rumors that despite his great personal references he wasn't quite kosher, like they say.

"But you can't throw away a huge account on

mere suspicion. So my dad hired a forensic accountant. That's an accountant who investigates where money is hidden. They are used a lot in divorce cases when the husband tries to keep from paying what he should to his wife. We never learned what his accountant had found for he suddenly disappeared. Most of him that is. His head washed up on the Long Island shoreline near his home."

I felt as if I had been punched in the stomach. Erika was describing the most astonishing events in a calm matter-of-fact voice, like she might tell of a school event, "I got an A on my social studies test," except here she was describing murder.

She had been hunched forward and looking down as she spoke. Almost as if she was talking to herself and trying to accept–to really accept–the reality of what had happened. Which, even with the fantastic detail of the severed head, I had promised to accept as fact too, along with whatever else she might tell me.

So, maybe from feeling a little more relaxed since she had gained an ally, Erika then leaned back against the sofa, sprawled out her legs, took a deep breath and continued speaking.

"My dad might have been a little naive for he accepted the police explanation. That this accountant had dabbled in drug sales on the side and was done in by a Mexican gang. Because my father didn't really know this accountant, he accepted their story. But when the next accountant he hired also turned up dead—this time after being hit by a stolen truck—my dad contacted a friend of Ivan who works in the Treasury Department. It was from her that he learned who 'Z' really was. He wasn't a nice guy at all.

"'Z' started out as a small time drug dealer in Turkey, just one of many along the long road from the poppy fields of Afghanistan to the final destination of Europe. Even as a youth he stood out for his ruthlessness. When his wife and two young children were being held for ransom, he found the location and, being unable to rescue them, killed them first and then the kidnappers. Then he killed the families of the kidnappers. Then he killed their friends. He showed them how hard he was, and what fear was like. He followed God's commandment to Joshua, 'Kill, kill, and spare not.'"

"My father explained him to me. He said that 'Z' is not a simple brute but that he has a philosophy of life. Had he been a soldier he might be greatly honored for he has the qualities of fearlessness and cunning and determination which are admired in the military.

"Those who know him have said that he does believe in a personal God and a Devil but refuses to allow either to interfere with his business. In a sense, he is even a fair fighter for he always gives warning to his enemies. But he doesn't value human life. Just as a typhoon feels free to kill both people and animals, he follows the gospel of frightfulness into his criminal activities and despises those who don't act similarly.

"He feels that few can distinguish between the real and the pretense, and his friendly appearance has kept him safe. The major feature of his life is his ruthlessness, and the rage he feels for those who oppose him. For them, he has but one rule: 'You will not live, and you will suffer terribly before dying.

"His mind is one of complete evil. If he wrote a letter saying how he viewed the world, anyone reading it would go crazy though 'Z' isn't crazy.

"People think of others as being insane if they act in an exaggerated manner like Maureen did today, screaming in the cafeteria. But 'Z' isn't like that for he's always calm. Have you ever read about the Nazis and World War Two?"

"A little, but it's too depressing."

"Well Himmler, head of the Nazi SS, told his troops that they should not get excited about killing the

Jews in the concentration camps, that they must never enjoy it. 'Z' is like that. He would have been a Nazi if he could ever tolerate being part of a group."

I loved Erika but her story was getting to me. "OK," I said, "I get it. Your dad made the mistake of getting into business with a guy he shouldn't have. The guy lost money so presumably their business relationship is over. 'Z' is a monster. So how does all of this involve you?"

The sun was setting and the view of her lawn was gorgeous. Flowers and old shade trees and empty lawn chairs with only an occasional shotgun carrying guard walking by to disturb the image.

"But it's not over," she said. "I guess I haven't been clear. 'Z' lost money and he's not a good loser. He sees my father as having caused him pain so he wants to inflict more pain onto him. That's why he had my sister and mother raped and murdered. That's what he plans to have done to me, and soon. He won't kill my father quickly. He wants him to suffer for the rest of the short life which he plans for him, to make up for what he has done.

"Do you know what I miss most about my sister and mother?"

I felt so shocked by what Erika had told me that I

was unable to speak. I shook my head.

"I remember their voices. I can no longer see their faces but I still remember the love in their voices."

Chapter 8

Erika wanted me to sleep over. She must be feeling afraid, I thought. After hearing her story I was afraid too though I knew that living it was far worse.

I called my mom, who said that my staying over with Erika would be OK. My parents knew her father and, with his security system, they couldn't imagine me being safer. This was how I felt that morning but after hearing Erika's story I no longer did.

But, like with Maureen at Rillston Hospital, I really still couldn't imagine what these girls were feeling. I made sympathetic statements but that was being polite. I simply had never experienced, as they had, the death of someone close to them.

My grandmother died several years before and I did love her, but she was elderly and ill so her death, if one may so describe it, might be considered a blessing. And being a devout Mormon and considering her pain and age, death wasn't something that she feared. She was more afraid of losing her independence.

But for a child to have their loved ones be raped and murdered, with the prospect of this happening to them, must create unimaginable feelings. How could one live with this? I didn't know but trusted that Mother Marie might. Perhaps by calling upon Obatala, the wisest of all the Orisha Gods, or Orula, the diviner, who can read the past, present, and future. If we couldn't survive with their help, then Erika and I must indeed be lost.

Living in Erika's house must be what living in the White House is like, I thought. Whatever you ask for is there, or gotten quickly. But we weren't hungry. After Erika told me her story, or horror movie you might call it, we just moped around. I offered to do her nails but she wasn't into it and considering what she was feeling I wouldn't have trusted her to do mine.

So Erika lay on the chaise lounge in what had been her mother's home study and held one of her mother's medical books before her. It wasn't upside down as Maureen had held her book but I didn't think that an anatomy book held much interest for Erika.

I managed to find a book which I did get interested in. Considering Erika and her father's threat from 'Z' I could likely find none better.

It was a psychology book which didn't describe criminals as being monsters who were born that way and couldn't be changed but tried to understand them. The psychologist wrote that criminals could be changed into law-abiding people in four ways. By getting the criminal to associate punishment—going to jail—with their crime of theft or rape or murder. Thereafter, when they were about to do it, the thought of punishment would enter their mind. Or by getting the criminal to reason about their criminal behavior so that they came to realize that it led to disaster. Then the criminal would decide beforehand to not do what they ordinarily would have done when being in a tempting situation. Like when a former rapist is alone in an elevator with a woman. Another change would be for the criminal to examine their behavior morally, to consider the pain it causes others, perhaps their parents or wife.

I was excited about these ideas, and felt they might apply to 'Z.' But when I explained them to Erika her comment was less than enthusiastic though her tone was kind since she recognized that I was trying to help her.

"Margaret, for a very smart girl, you sometimes talk like an idiot. 'Z' is a monster. One does not reason with monsters. They must be destroyed."

But perhaps even monsters can be changed, I wondered, this being the moral of a story which Mother Marie had told me.

Being unable to gain love, the powerful witch,

Okana, cursed all those about her and her soul filled with darkness: "If I can't be happy, then no one shall." She turned her witchcraft to evil things, creating poverty and storms and fires. Cows no longer gave milk, and children died.

The townspeople sought the diviner Mofá and made offering. Then Okana's curses were turned back onto herself. She became weak and ill and powerless and left the land of her birth, crying for the love she had lost and the evil she created. She cried because she did not know what else to do. Finally, Okana had no home or magic, and lay in a mud puddle in the street. A finely dressed man stood above her. "I have been searching for you Okana, for it is not well that a woman with your talents should be lying in the street."

He asked her help in caring for his dying father. Despite her sadness, Okana cared for the elderly man with the kindness and tenderness which she would have given to her own father. And when he passed on to that place of safety which is free of worries, his son, Salako', fell in love with Okana, and they married and had children and grandchildren and knew love and she had everything that she ever wanted.

Along with this story I remembered something else which Mother Marie had told me: the law of magic:

that like attracts like. Thus things which have been in contact with each other continue to affect each other long after their contact is broken. That our egun, or ancestors, still exist and look over us, a concept which is no different from the angels which other religions believe in. And if the police were helpless, I thought, maybe the spirits of my grandmother and Erika's mother and sister still existed, and could help us.

About six-thirty, Erika said she had cooking to do. Perhaps feeling that, despite the live-in help, this was her responsibility since her mother's death. So, as with all the other activities she did, she became a great cook. I'm smart too but don't have the patience. Erika would as soon serve frozen or canned lasagna to her father as I would be to cook it from scratch. We may now be sisters but this big difference will always exist between us.

She and the live-in cook decided on the evening meal. One similarity between Erika and me was that we were both into healthy, low-fat eating. So that night's meal included fish fillets with ginger marmalade sauce, Vietnamese fisherman's soup, and, for dessert, fruity oatmeal bars which had a simple recipe: quick-cooking oats, cinnamon, cloves, chopped dates and apricots, unsweetened apple sauce in place of butter, and a tablespoon of sugar though exactly why this was added I had no idea.

The fish entree arose from her experiments with cooking and was so simple to prepare that even I could have done it. It involves spreading ginger marmalade, which is a British favorite, along with Dijon mustard and vinegar, onto the fish and then baking it for five or six minutes.

The soup had both a sweet and tart flavor with about a dozen ingredients including fish stock, lime juice, sugar, garlic, onions, carrots, water chestnuts, shrimp and fish, tomato, bean sprouts, cilantro leaves, and green chile. Once you put together all the ingredients, the cooking time was only twenty five minutes.

The soup came from a recipe which Abram, her personal bodyguard, had brought back from his recent trip to Vietnam. Abram had been introduced to Erika's father by Ivan, who was his uncle. Both had been born in Russia and Abram's name was the Russian version of Abraham.

Like Ivan, Abram was big but very light on his feet. He was also a very good dancer, Erika had told me. When no boy at a country club dance invited her to dance, for the sight of Abram would quickly end any romantic notions which a teenager might have about

Erika, Abram had danced with her. Which made the girls there jealous for Abram is a very good looking guy. Think of a thirty-four-year-old Justin Bieber with hair so blond that it's almost white and eyes so deeply blue that they almost glint. Unfortunately, unlike his uncle Ivan, Abram was married and had two young sons.

Abram had learned English in Russia and spoke it as well or badly as I did. After college he worked in a self-defense school (he said) or the Russian Federal Security Service (which is their secret service, Erika said). I tend to believe Erika's version for one day Abram told me about the training he taught. It was an Israeli import called Krav Maga which means "battle contact."

"There are three rules," he told me. "To counter-attack as soon as possible, or to attack first; to attack your opponent's most vulnerable points such as the eyes and throat and groin; and to keep attacking until your enemy is down. Meanwhile you must maintain awareness of your surroundings to look for further threats, objects which could be used for defense and attack, and escape routes."

During his Russian training, students who were well-padded in protective outfits fought each other until they were exhausted.

Holding these comforting thoughts, Erika and I set the dining room table and then went upstairs to dress. Dinners at this house were always casual but dressy. Erika changed into an Ondade Mar handkerchief layered dress in swirling acid colors and matching sandals. Being four inches shorter than me, I couldn't borrow any of her clothes so I settled for the usual shirt and jeans I always wear and added Erika's flame COVERGIRL LIPCOVER which matched my hair.

Her father, Hamilton's ("call me Harry") business meeting ran over-time so it wasn't until eight-fifteen that we ate.

The dining room was large and lit by several chandeliers over the long table. The deep red walls, dark polished wood furniture, and formal place settings gave it an elegant, moody, traditional look. The metal shutters had been closed so the evening sunset could not be seen.

Despite the tension in the room, for bullet-proof shutters and armed bodyguards do not add gaiety to any surroundings, Erika's father kept the conversation going. Ivan and Abram ate quietly, occasionally looking about the room though there was nothing unusual to see.

Erika's father asked how her day had been and

then spoke of his business meeting. She had apparently taken the place of confidante which his wife had held.

He was worried about the huge amount of money which people were willing to pay for tech stocks which were earning little or no profit. It was believed that each of them would become the next Apple or Google despite the recession, which was continuing. He told of how one house in Silicon Valley had been purchased for two million dollars over its three million dollar asking price despite there being a plumbing leak in the kitchen. Even higher offers were made after the sales contract was signed.

"They forget how much risk is involved in these companies. Owners who own companies which are too highly valued are now buying stock in other companies for far too much money.

"One tech company was bought for thirty five million dollars six years ago and just sold for five hundred and eighty million dollars. It has yet to earn a profit. The cuckoos have come out of the clock. You know the old saying about what happens to those who forget the past..."

"They are doomed to repeat it," Erika said, completing his sentence as perhaps her mother had done, and he patted her hand affectionately.

Erika's father tried to include me in the conversation. He asked about my father's Lyme disease and whether he expected to fully re-open his law practice. He had been kind enough to refer a client to my father several months before, for completion of the well-paying, easily done paperwork task of transferring the ownership of a yacht to its newly retired former hedge fund owner.

I told him that my father was a bit better, and about the disabilities which Lyme disease might cause. That it was sad how a tiny insect bite could lead to such grave consequences.

Then Erika's father said something which made me think. He said that it was often the littlest things which bring big men down and protect others. Could this apply to 'Z,' I wondered. Could a tiny event protect Erika, her father, and me, since I had entered their lives and now shared the danger of knowing the truth about 'Z.'

If Babaluaiye, my Orisha God husband, had seen fit to heal me of my illness, then would other Orisha Gods protect me: perhaps old Obatalá, with his wisdom and the coolness of the elderly, or Ochosi, the hunter, to render justice?

I became so lost in this idea that my soup spoon

dropped as it was half-way to my lips. Both Erika and her father smiled though I felt embarrassed. The soup stained the patterned table cloth and brought another memory: Mother Marie's story of how the smallest and most defenseless creature became powerful and feared.

The spider was once the weakest creature of all who walked the Earth. In desperation the spider sought help from Obatalá, saying, "I am the weakest of creatures and cannot defend myself. I am always hungry for I am too tiny to catch my prey."

Obatalá replied: "But though you are small you have sharp fangs, and in your mouth is a poison so powerful that it will kill huge men."

"But I am small and so slow that when someone sees me they run away or smash me."

Then Obatalá said, "I will help you but first you must bring me something I need."

"Anything!" the spider replied.

The spider went into town and brought a white silk handkerchief from a seller of cloth at the market, pulling it in her tiny fangs back to Obatalá. Then Obatala placed the fine silk cloth about the spider and told her to sleep and that when she awoke she would discover her fate.

When the spider awoke the next morning the

awnings of the front porch were covered in fine silk. Within it was a fly which had been caught in the spider's web, and on which it could feast.

And at that moment all the events of the past hour seemed to come together though I could not yet see how: being able to gain help from ancestors; the Law of Magic, that like attracts like, and the kindness of Erika's father; his comment that it is often the smallest things which bring big men down and protect others; and Mother Marie's story of how the spider became powerful.

I now knew what Erika and I had to do. We had to spin our web to destroy a wasp.

Chapter 9

I was tired and I expected that Erika was too but the dinner wore on. Her father needed to talk and relax and she, and I it now seemed, were trusted. I was sure that he also trusted his bodyguards, particularly Ivan and Abram. But these were employees and even at my young age I knew that one could never fully relax with them.

So I tried to keep from drooping and listened as he described his day. Not the financial deals he made for these were, of course, confidential. But the personalities of the people he met and how he negotiated with them. I said nothing except to make appreciative comments. How could I do otherwise considering my family's poverty and my father's legal profession, from which what I learned had nothing to do with Wall Street.

But Erika did make comments and her father took these seriously. She was very smart and was growing up in a deal making family. Her mother had been a surgeon who began a surgical equipment company. Only a fool—which her father was certainly not—would not listen to Erika.

"I did a good deed today," he said.

"What was that?" Erika asked.

"I let someone in on a big deal and so will make less on it."

"You must have had a very good reason for that," Erika said.

"Tell me what it is," he replied, and I realized that his stories were intended to educate Erika, just like the patakis, or sacred stories of Mother Marie, were intended to educate to.

"Was it because you liked him?" Erika asked with a smile.

Her father recognized that he was being teased. "Personal feelings don't enter into business contracts except in extreme situations like if a potential partner is dishonest."

"I'll bet you a quarter that I know why you made that deal."

"You're on."

"Make it a half dollar."

Erika's father smiled again. "You're still on."

"You're a conservative investor and wanted to spread the risk of the investment. When you place part of it on others' shoulders you reduce your potential loss. You'll make a smaller profit if things turn out well but if the deal goes badly you won't lose as much. You can also make many more deals with less money and increase your odds of a really big payout."

Harry beamed and handed her a dollar. "My daughter."

"Our bet was for fifty cents. I'll tidy your office tomorrow."

This was some pair, I thought.

Harry continued his lesson. "Another problem. A hedge fund manager was approached by two men. They offered him ownership in a company but at a price which would have placed them at a great disadvantage while giving the buyer a huge profit. Should he proceed with the contract? Margaret, what do you think."

"I don't know," I said. "Maybe they were making a mistake."

"Erika?"

"He shouldn't make the deal without conducting an extensive investigation of the sellers and the company first. And even then he should pray a lot. It might be that, for some personal reason, they needed the money then or are simply making a mistake. But it is more likely that they are setting up a fraud, selling you well-wrapped garbage."

"Right on," Harry said, with a bigger smile. "And you can forget about cleaning my office tomorrow. What is the lesson to draw from this?"

"You should always distrust any apparent mistake being made by your opponent. It may be their mistake but it is more likely their attempt to conceal their plan to deceive you. It is not reasonable to assume that your opponent—which is anyone who you deal with in business negotiations—is so careless.

"One should always follow the advice from *Machiavelli's Discourses*: 'any error on the part of an enemy should make us suspicious.'"

Wow! I thought, does this girl really need *my* help?

Chapter 10

Our presence gave Erika's father a second wind and he seemed inclined to remain talking for hours longer. This indicated, I felt, his loneliness and need for a wife. Maybe I could help him find one.

My Aunt Lena, was a great businesswoman and wife, as her two (deceased) husbands had found. Could Erika's father be her third? Aunt Lena was still young enough to have the children she always wanted. Together, considering their good lucks and intelligence, their children might be as exceptional as Erika.

But my idea of matchmaking was just a passing fantasy: even this fourteen-year-old virgin knew her real world limitations.

By eleven our fatigue had become obvious even to Erika's father. So we said our good-nights and went to bed.

While there were many empty bedrooms, I thought that Erika might have wanted me to sleep in her room. But, though exhausted, the talk with her father seemed to have strengthened her and she no longer seemed afraid. She offered me a bedroom down the hall from hers. The one closest to her had been her sister's and no one was permitted to use it anymore.

I couldn't object. While my bedroom at home was nice, that of a typical teenager, those in this house were luxurious. The one Erika gave me was large, about thirty feet long and twenty feet wide. It had an adjoining bathroom nearly half the size, which was plenty big. There was a huge Jacuzzi bathtub and adjoining shower.

The bed was a queen size four-poster Louis V-style with an embroidered headboard and footboard. Tapestry chairs and cushions completed the style. The pillows and sheets were pale pink. The matching small flower patterns on the walls and ceiling added to the room's sense of elegance.

Beside the bed were night tables with a lamp atop each. These were tall and provided enough light for reading or, using the dimmer switch, for putting on makeup. On one side of the room was a chest for clothes or whatever.

There were large French doors which opened onto a terrace though Erika warned me not to open them. If I did, an alarm would go off and armed bodyguards would burst into my room. So if you do decide to open the terrace door, she suggested impishly, put some clothes on first.

There was also a dressing table which could be

used as a desk, and a sofa surrounded by club chairs. On the desk was a MacBook Pro. Unlike in my family, the cost of laptops and Internet connection was no problem. Before leaving, Erika reminded me of the major house rule: if you hear an alarm, run immediately to the security room on the floor.

"What if I'm naked?" I asked jokingly.

"You'll find coveralls there," she said without a smile. Erika was serious; I promised to take short showers.

Being shorter than me, none of her clothes fit me. But she gave me packets of disposable underwear and socks, adding that I could do without a bra. Considering that I was a small "A" and she was a "C", she was right, though I could have done without her comment.

The bathroom held a unisex bathrobe, hair dryer, and anything else I might need. Staying at Erika's home was like being in a luxury hotel.

I thought of checking my Facebook page for messages but was too tired. So I stripped to my panties and fell under the covers, falling asleep almost immediately.

I read somewhere that psychologists believe that dreams occur just before you wake up in the morning but mine must have occurred in the middle of the night.

In my dream Randy and I were married and living in the apartment complex where both Mother Marie and Aunt Lena lived. I was cooking dinner, putting Chinese take-out on the table which is how it will likely be, when the doorbell rang. I opened it and faced machete wielding, stocking masked thugs. Randy heard my scream, came running toward me, and was cut down. They had begun to rip off my clothes when a peeling alarm followed by a loud but calm, female voice awoke me. "Attention! Attention! There is an intruder. Go to your secure location." The alarm and message repeated over and over.

While I awoke in a fright, I realized that though I had been dreaming, the alarm was real. I followed Erika's advice and ran barefoot to the security room. Erika had beat me there. She sat calmly on the bench holding a shotgun, wearing a coverall and sneakers. Even dressed in these and without makeup she looked beautiful. She nodded toward a rack in the corner. I chose a coverall and sneakers and dressed. Then we waited without speaking.

She had locked the door after I arrived. There was no more to do until reinforcements came. She handed me a pistol and explained how to use it.

"It's a twelve shot Makatov PMM. It has what is

called a double-action/single-action operating system. After loading, you charge the pistol by pulling back the slide. You can carry it safely with the hammer down and the safety engaged. In order to fire, the safety lever is pushed down to the 'fire' position, after which you squeeze the trigger to fire the gun.

"Squeezing the trigger for the first shot also cocks the hammer so the first shot will be harder than the rest. Then the firing and cycling of the action re-cocks the hammer so you can fire it in what is called 'single action' with a short, light trigger squeeze.

"The PMM's operation is semi-automatic. It will fire as quickly as you can squeeze the trigger. Spent cartridges are ejected away to your right and rear. When the safety is engaged, the hammer drops from the cocked position. The safety lever has a notch that blocks the hammer from striking the firing pin. This is the only safe way to lower the hammer.

"You won't have to remember all this," she said, as she slipped the magazine into the gun and cocked it. She disengaged the safety and handed it to me. "Keep your finger off the trigger and don't shoot unless I do. Don't point the gun at anyone unless you intend to shoot them. If you do shoot, shoot to kill and don't miss!"

She indicated a large red button on the wall

closest to us. "Don't press that button. If they try to break down the door, pressing it will explode multiple tasers in a twenty degree arc outside. Like a remote controlled land mine. We'll know when to use it by seeing who's outside on the closed circuit camera screen next to it."

This isn't like any hotel I ever heard of, I thought, as we sat and waited for an attack, our rescue, or whatever.

Erika offered me bottled water and my choice of granola bars but I had lost my appetite. She pointed to a portable toilet behind a screen in the corner in case I needed to use it. Despite the weirdness of this event, Erika was behaving with her usual consideration for others.

About ten minutes later (I had left my watch in the room) we saw Erika's father and Abram on the TV screen outside and she received a coded message over the intercom. She opened the heavy steel door. Her father was dressed in jeans and a T-shirt. Abram wore a black ski jacket and pants. Both held guns at their side.

Her father's gun looked something like a rifle but not any which I had ever seen. It had a weird looking shoulder stock, shaped like an "L" and the trigger housing was just as odd. Like something out of a science fiction movie.

Abram's gun was just as strange. Though being similar to the one which Erika had given me, it had a long bulky attachment to the barrel. Both smiled at the sight of Erika's shotgun and my pistol.

"Just a test. You both did well," her father remarked. "Go back to bed."

We intended to but were too wired up to sleep. So we went downstairs for a snack. Erika toasted bagels and I poured the juice.

"What kind of gun did your father have? I've never seen anything like it."

"It's a forty-five caliber Kriss Super V Vector, the civilian model of a Swiss military weapon. It's his three thousand dollar toy. My father is a lousy shot."

I thought for a moment. "Abram is a good looking guy. It's too bad that he's married."

Erika just nodded.

"What kind of gun was he holding?"

Erika hesitated before speaking. "It's a Makarov, like the one you held but is a PB model, a Pistolet Besshumnyy, or "silent pistol." Abram was a member of the Vympel, which was the best Russian anti-terrorist unit. He resigned along with many others after the fall of the old Soviet Union when it was integrated into the police force. They felt this action humiliated them.

"He speaks three languages fluently and is expert at protecting diplomats. That's why my father hired him as a bodyguard. He helped him to become an American citizen."

"That's an impressive resume. But why does he carry such a strange looking pistol?"

"He prefers it. His Russian unit carried it when they were behind enemy lines, and it's a favorite of Russian spies. The fat barrel is a silencer. It quiets the sound of the shot so the enemy can be killed without anyone hearing."

Chapter 11

I awoke at twelve thirty in the afternoon, wondering whether the events of the night had been real or just another bad dream. Over the years I had occasional scary dreams but they didn't really frighten me since I knew that everyone did. They were just part of being human, the instructor of my babysitting class had told us.

"Dreams are like mystery movies which tell you how you see your life. Like if you are worried about someone's health you might dream that they are dying. Or if you dream that you are in danger it only means that there are scary things going on inside of you. Maybe you are about to try something new and it frightens you."

"Let's say that there is real danger in your life," I asked, "Like being an undercover FBI agent. Wouldn't that give you nightmares too with their purpose being to warn you that your life is in danger?"

"Yes," the teacher agreed. "But that isn't the kind of job which most people have so their danger usually relates to something more personal. For teenagers this is usually about dating or their future or their parents."

This explanation of nightmares still made sense to me. I wondered what mine had been trying to tell me and sensed that it wasn't good. But this thought did give me a good idea: to try to get a job babysitting.

Since my father became disabled and unable to work, money had become a big issue in my life. We still had enough food to eat and a nice place to live but I felt crippled. Teenagers need a few dollars to live: to be able to buy a bottle of juice or to use the ferry to get to one of the two Greenwich town beaches which are on islands.

I never mentioned this to my parents since they had enough to worry about. But I carried this worry along with me, like the figure in Samuel Taylor Coleridge's poem, *The Rime of the Ancient Mariner*, which we read in Honors English.

It's a long poem but several lines, for whatever reason, had remained in my memory and I repeated them aloud. I was glad that I was alone though I knew that Erika never made fun of anyone.

> He prayeth best, who loveth best
> All things both great and small;
> For the dear God who loveth us,
> He made and loveth all.

Love is what is most important the poem insisted. And though my family was poor, I knew that I was loved. So, I concluded, my present poverty was just another of the problems which everyone has as they go through life.

After thinking this I became less gloomy.

I showered in my luxurious bathroom, dressed in the disposable underwear which Erika gave me and the jeans and shirt which I had arrived with, and went downstairs for breakfast feeling happy. Hadn't my English teacher said, quoting Plato, that, "The most effective kind of education is that a child should play amongst lovely things."

Erika said that her father had been long gone, to a business breakfast meeting. No matter what time he went to sleep, he still would be out of the house by eight at the latest. I felt groggy and envied his energy.

Ivan sat with us, along with a tall woman in her late twenties who had just arrived. She was dressed in a white blouse and white linen pants and loafers. Erika introduced her as, Ava, her father's friend.

Ava had a quick smile and seemed kindly, almost motherly. Though the food was set on a side table, like at hotel buffets, she offered to serve me and I let her. It's always nice to be waited on!

Apart from the cold salmon, a dish which I love but is far too expensive to be found in our kitchen, the food was little different from that in my home: oatmeal, fruit, bread and bagels, juice, milk, and the coffee which we and most other Mormons never drink.

Ava described a trip to New York which she had taken with Erika's father and I quickly got the message that she was more than his "friend" and would welcome becoming Erika's next mother. A task which Erika later told me would never happen.

"Ava's sweet and I could love her like a sister but she's not smart enough for my dad. He needs someone he can share his ideas with. Though she is elegant enough and has the big breasts which he likes in women."

Months before I would have been shocked by such a frank comment. But being friends with Erika had changed me, and her accurate sense of others wasn't new. Though he lacked her father's billions, my dad's comments had the same quality like with every good lawyer. And, I again thought, if my Aunt Lena and her father married they would be an unbeatable combination.

I decided that my best adviser on how to make money would be Erika, the daughter of the richest person in America's wealthiest town. So we spent the next hour discussing it.

"You're too young for a real job but if you were older my dad would hire you," she said, though I wondered if her words didn't reflect only her kind nature.

"But I just turned fourteen and need a job now."

"So you shouldn't waste time looking for a typical job: one which a person who is older than you can do in a standard business. What knowledge or experiences have you that others don't have and which would be considered valuable and worth paying for?"

I thought. I had been doing law research using the library's computer for five years for my father since he got sick; and I earned a Red Cross babysitting certificate two years before.

I also, along with Randy, had some experience as a burglar as I described in *Margaret of Greenwich*, but I didn't see how this could be used in a legitimate job.

I shared these thoughts with Erika.

"You could help a criminal lawyer with their law research," she suggested.

"Yes, but they'd still consider me a kid."

Erika nodded. "So we fall back on babysitting. Many parents here would welcome getting time free from their kids and your family is well-known. But you won't be a babysitter. You'll be their manager."

This is how my need to get a few dollars turned into The Greenwich Babysitting Registry, LLC ("LLC" stands for "corporation", like "Inc."). And Erika knew how to set this up.

"We'll have to establish a corporation to protect my family and yours against being sued if something bad happens. Then the corporation would be sued and a person can't lose more than the money in the corporation.

"There are different kinds of corporation but we'll make ours a Limited Liability Corporation. It's a 'corporation lite' meaning that there is less red tape though it still has the same legal protections of a corporation and that's what we are interested in. Also that the business sounds professional."

"We're underage. How can we open a corporation?"

Erika thought for a moment. "I'll ask Abram to be the statutory agent. This means that he'll receive all of the legal notices. I'll have Ivan be the other name we need for that of a non-owner manager.

"You'll own ninety percent of the stock since the business was your idea and I'll own ten percent. You'll be the treasurer and handle the money and do the hiring. One of my dad's accountants will handle the taxes but we'll have all the fun. I'll download and print out the state corporate forms from the Internet now."

Though I objected to the stock split, feeling that Erika was being far too generous, she insisted on it even as I wondered if our business might not soon become yet another of America's recent bankruptcies.

Erika is a great organizer when she gets an idea but had she considered the obvious problem which our business would face and why no one else was doing it: the need to find Greenwich teenagers who would be willing to work as babysitters.

Living in the wealthiest town in America, few of them needed money. Those seeking a job did so for the feeling of independence and pride it gained them. But they would certainly look down upon babysitting. That isn't work which you would want your friends to know you did. But, being poor, I didn't mind. And, as my dad always said, all honest jobs are good ones, to which I add, particularly today when a job is so hard to find.

Erika is a demon for details so within an hour the necessary papers had been completed, signed by the smiling Ivan and Abram, and faxed to the office of the Connecticut Secretary of State. The one hundred twenty dollar fee was paid with Erika's credit card. She said that it would represent her stock purchase in our new corporation.

Erika was no typical thirteen-year-old girl, I thought. She was certainly her billionaire father's daughter!

Chapter 12

We began working. What I knew personally about babysitting came from my experience with my own babysitters, who were either my older sister, Melody, or our long-time family friend, Sergeant Alamo of the Greenwich Police Department; or what I had learned from babysitting my sister, Melanie, who was four years younger than me.

All my knowledge could be put into just two sentences: unless the child is doing something dangerous or destructive, let them do it; and give them whatever they want to eat unless it is poisonous.

Many parents would laugh at my simple rules though it is exactly what they do. Except in the crazy families where parents battle their children over who is the boss, which sometimes leads to child abuse and worse.

So as far as I was concerned, being a babysitter was just being a good parent though, of course, I would never say that to the parents who hired us. It would make the job seem too simple and force us to lower our prices.

Instead, I planned to emphasize that all of The

Register's babysitters had completed a basic first aid course and been interviewed by the company's management, which consisted of me and Erika.

Being able to use her name to attract business would have been great for many parents would welcome any kind of relationship, distant though it may be, with her billionaire father. But Erika had been firm: her name could not be used. Her father was busy and didn't need to answer calls from our disappointed customers, which we hoped never to have. For this reason we used as a business address that of the house which I will inherit when I turn twenty-one.

We made up a checklist of questions for the babysitters who we hoped to find. Have you taken a basic first aid class? Have you ever been a babysitter for relatives or at your church's nursery? What times and days of the week will you be available? Do you have transportation to a Greenwich location, either by your parents or by bike? What is your grade average?

I wondered about the last question but Erika believed that a teenager who got poor grades might have a problem concentrating and so could not guarantee the safety of the child they were babysitting. I wasn't so sure. My boyfriend, Randy, is a genius and always gets the highest grades in school. But his head is usually in the clouds and I'd never trust any child in his care. Also because he's not savvy enough about relationships: the child would twist Randy about their finger.

But I went along with Erika's notion. She was, after all, the business genius of our school. And she did think of things which I never would have, like the importance of being treated with respect by the parents. Just because someone was hiring you didn't mean that they could treat you however they wanted.

Keeping our babysitters safe was Erika's biggest worry. Because of the murder and rape of her mother and sister, and she being a prime kidnapping target, she always worried about personal safety. She had read on Google News of real estate agents, usually young pretty women, who went to empty houses with men who said that they were interested in buying them. The women were then raped or worse. Women who, in this terrible economy, were just trying to help their families survive and too easily taken in by a sweet voice. This would not happen to our girls, Erika vowed.

This produced Rule Number One in our employee manual: if anything about the child's parents makes you uneasy, you are to quickly leave their house and call us. We will then decide whether to call the police, and also pay you for two hours of your time so that it wasn't entirely wasted. Rule Number Two was that every girl must carry a cell phone with its location finder on.

But we didn't want to rely only on the girl's judgment for we knew that some girls weren't street wise. So we planned to screen the parents too. I had lived in Greenwich all my life and met many families. Erika had been in Greenwich for just five years but, through her many civic activities and the meetings she attended with her father, also knew many of the residents.

Those who neither of us had met, we would check out through an Internet company which her father had a contract with. It told everything about a person: their education; where they had lived previously; if they had ever been arrested or sued, even their income.

Erica, her current bodyguard, Abram, and me would visit the homes of parents who neither of us had met. I felt sure that the sight of Abram would impress them. Think of a guy with the build of Arnold Schwarzenegger but younger and being much better looking.

But having Abram along did concern me. I was afraid that more than a few of the mothers would prefer for him to babysit them and lose interest in buying our service. Still, our babysitters always had to be safe and their parents must believe this.

We never considered hiring boys. Teaching a boy to be an acceptable evening's date was hard enough. Turning him into a good parent, even for just a few hours, we both considered impossible. Also, we doubted that many boys would take orders from a female boss—even if she was paying them!

You're probably wondering how we could think of something so ordinary as babysitting just hours after we sat holding a shotgun and pistol and feared being raped and murdered. This isn't easy to explain but maybe hearing a story which Abram told us, from his experience as a Russian officer, will help.

I'm warning you now! It is scary and not one which you'd want to tell your friends.

It involved a terrorist attack on a school which went very wrong on both sides. The terrorists took over a school and held eleven hundred children and teachers as hostage. They said that they would release them if their demands were met. But they made the big mistake of asking for the wrong people to negotiate with, and the government made their own big mistake of having many generals who either weren't talking to each other or disagreed about what to do.

Bombs had been planted throughout the building

and the children and teachers weren't given food or water. They were made to stand all the time and some fainted. The temperature was so hot that many took all their clothes off. Meanwhile, outside the building, their parents were yelling for the military to do something and some had brought their own guns to help. As you can imagine, there was much confusion.

Finally, the soldiers attacked the building with tanks and rockets and machine guns. Over three hundred people were killed including nearly two hundred of the children. Many were burned alive. It was not the happy ending like you see in those old time western movies with the cavalry riding in to the rescue and music blaring. Nine soldiers in Abram's unit were killed. His young daughter was killed too.

Abram said that for months afterward he and his wife felt like they were "dead people walking." Still, they managed to care for their other two children. That was when Abram decided to leave Russia and contacted Ivan, who arranged for a job with Erika's father.

That was also how Erika and I felt that morning: like the walking dead. We were both expecting to be raped and murdered since I too knew about "Z" and we had become, in both of our minds, sisters.

So to try to forget this we threw ourselves into our

babysitting business, now having become just another two of the other "walking dead" who awaited "Z"'s terror.

Chapter 13

We really threw ourselves into our babysitting business. We decided that our first task was to write two handouts: one for hiring babysitters and the other to find customers. Since I was the better writer this job was mine. It read as follows.

"The Greenwich Babysitting Registry, LLC is your resource for finding trained babysitters in Greenwich. The girls we provide have completed basic first aid classes and are experienced with young children. Our fees are reasonable. We welcome your telephone call so that we may discuss our services in detail."

We signed the notice using Abram's name as the president and mine as the manager.

The notice to recruit babysitters was less formal.

"Girls: Want to do a good deed, have fun, and make money for your spare time too? Call Margaret at the Greenwich Babysitters Registry LLC. We work with only the best Greenwich families."

"Have fun?" Erika asked.

"Many kids are."

"What about those that aren't?"

"That's why they're being paid. If taking care of

kids was always fun then babysitting wouldn't be called work."

"As mine, yours, and every parent says about working."

I didn't reply. Some smart comments don't deserve a response. Besides, I thought, Erika's bitchiness was probably caused by the crazy night which we were both trying to forget.

We printed two hundred of each form and spent the next few hours being driven about Greenwich by Abram and posting them. All of the shopkeepers we approached were nice enough to let us leave them in their stores.

I left Erika a little before three for that was the day which I usually spent with my other best friend, Hillary. She was still mooning about her "beloved," former president Bill Clinton who lived fifteen miles away, just across the New York State border in Chappaqua. Though their love affair existed only in her mind, I wondered how soon it would be before she took the plunge and biked over.

Hillary lay on her bed, reading the latest biography of Bill Clinton. If they got together she would know more about him than any other girl did about her lover, I thought. With this came another train of thought: *Bill Clinton, her lover, their baby, my company's babysitter?*

"Hillary, you need money, don't you?" I began.

"Always." While both of her parents worked and so her family was financially far better off than mine, they based Hillary's allowance on her grades. An "A" average, which was her usual since she was really smart, was worth forty dollars a week. But after becoming fixated on *her Bill* her grades had, like they say, gone into the toilet. For the past several months she had been surviving on money from soda can deposits. No Greenwich families bothered to return them and she had become a frequent, nightly visitor to their garbage bins.

I sometimes went with her but let her keep the money. The books she hungered for about pregnancy, breastfeeding, and Bill Clinton were not cheap. And sleeping with them clutched to her heart or, with the one containing Bill's picture between her legs, made it non-returnable to the library. Explaining to the librarian why a book so stank of Coty's Wild Mist required an imagination beyond even mine.

So I decided that Hillary would be a great recruit for our babysitting business. Besides needing money, all she now thought about was Bill and babies. If they ever did hook-up, their children would certainly be exceptional, I predicted.

I continued my sales pitch.

"Erika and I have started a babysitting business for Greenwich families. You'll be paid twelve dollars an hour and keep ten dollars of it. Two dollars goes to us for expenses. We will screen every family before you go. Are you interested?"

Hillary was desperate for money. A new audio book of Bill's was in the bookstore and she hungered for it.

"How soon can I do it?"

"As quickly as we get a customer. You're free most every day during the summer, aren't you?"

Hillary just nodded. Her eyes had that dreamy look it got when her fantasy life took off. I could imagine what she was thinking. Bill moaning to her: "My stunningly beautiful, younger Hillary, the mother of our son and future American president." The crazy thing about this was that if their son was ever born and became a presidential candidate, Aunt Lena, a Democratic fundraiser, would probably vote for him, and Erika and I would too. I returned to the business at hand.

"You've taken a first aid class haven't you?"

"At the Red Cross, and a lifeguard class too."

"Great! And you've done babysitting?"

"What do you think? I have three younger brothers."

"You're perfect!. As soon as we get a customer I'll call you. Our only rules are that you carry your cell phone with the location indicator on, and if you feel uncomfortable about anything at the home, you leave immediately and call us."

"What about getting paid?"

"We'll pay you for two hours no matter what."

"You've got a babysitter!"

I hesitated about saying what had to be said. I don't like hurting anyone and she was my friend too, sometimes flaky but still a good friend.

"Go easy on the perfume, no micro skirts, wear a bra, and if you're strapless, wear a sweater. The families want a babysitter, not a surrogate mother even if you would be a perfect candidate with your brains and beauty." With this statement I followed my Aunt Lena's management advice that when you criticize a worker, you should always add a compliment.

Hillary's clothes over the past school year had earned her a notable reputation. The girls called her "a slut," and the boys considered her "the girl you would most like to..." Well, you get the idea.

Hillary nodded and took my advice surprisingly well. Her eyes had become dreamy again: "Bill" was probably undressing her.

Chapter 14

I quickly learned the frustrating lesson of all new business owners: that customers arrive slowly. They may glance at your brochure, then pick it up and save it for future use. Or toss it when they get outside the store, not wanting the shop owner to see them wasting someone's effort. So for a week after our business opened there was nothing. No calls or letters, except for one from the Connecticut tax department reminding us of the need to pay our taxes every three months.

"The way things are going all we'll have is a loss," Erika remarked. She knew much more about business matters than me but also tended to be more pessimistic. I would be too if my older sister and mother had been murdered, I thought.

"Give it time," I said softly, and turned back to my book. It was a psychology book which I found in Erika's library and had probably belonged to her mother. It wasn't a book which I would ordinarily have picked up but our experience with Maureen had changed me. Now when someone did or said something puzzling I would try to figure out why instead of politely ignoring it as I had always done.

Maureen's behavior *was* puzzling. She seemed to look forward to our visits and smiled as we approached her, looking no different from any other friend our age. Thereafter, she would continue to behave as if she were a much younger child. Going along with any activity we suggested, and taking our hands as we walked as if we were sisters or friends. But when we arrived, whether at the pool or library or cafeteria, unless we actually took her hand and explained what we were doing, she would just sit there. As if she didn't know anything though, of course, considering that she was fourteen too, she must have known as much as us.

So she was acting "dependent" according to the psychology book I was reading. But the important question, and for this the book had no definite answer, was why?

What would cause a grown-up fourteen-year-old to behave like a child. I couldn't see either me or Erika (who would soon be fourteen) act like that. What had caused Maureen to do it? What caused her to become a child again?

About this, the book did have information which seemed right on. That being a grown-up had suddenly become too hard for her so she went back to being a child. This made sense. How many grown women could endure, at the same time, the death of both their parents and having a child too. I doubted that I could though Erika was surviving events just as bad. But Erika was unusual. Most girls, *most people*, were not as smart or as sturdy as she is. I didn't think that I was though she might disagree.

While doing Erika's nails, I shared my ideas about Maureen.

"Babysitting a fourteen-year-old baby is driving me crazy."

"Me too. Do you want to stop?"

"We can't just disappear. We promised my aunt and Maureen's doctor, and we might be more important to Maureen than it seems."

"We could talk to her."

"Her doctor told us that she doesn't talk." I said. But then I had a thought. "If she won't or can't answer questions, why don't we just keep talking about our stuff and from time to time ask her questions related to it. Like if we're talking about dating, ask her if she ever had a boyfriend who acted dumb. She must have."

"It's worth a shot."

That's what we did on our next visit. We had already planned our conversation. I would tell her about a science project which Randy was doing: using mild electrical charges on damaged cells to see if this promoted their healing. It seemed strange to me but Erika reminded me that some great medical discoveries have arisen in off-beat ways. Like the discovery of penicillin from what most would have considered a throwaway mold.

We arrived at the hospital in time to have a late breakfast with Maureen. Who, thankfully, still managed to eat. Sitting and eating at a cafeteria table with a non-eating friend would be almost too uncomfortable. But however Maureen behaved, I always enjoyed our visits to the Rillston Hospital cafeteria. Though there was always enough food in our house, I did miss the treats which I craved and which were available in the cafeteria without charge, like in many Silicon Valley companies.

The first time we were there, Erika commented on my food choices: always baked salmon, always whitefish sandwiches, always ice cream sandwiches. All were my favorites and usually unavailable to me. After hearing my explanation, she no longer commented. Erika was, as I have said, the kindest and most tactful girl I knew. Randy's parents had brought him up to be courteous, which was another reason I loved him, and Erika's parents had done an equally good job.

That day I chose the baked salmon with side

orders of spinach and broccoli and a whole-wheat bagel on the side. Unlike many teenagers, I love vegetables, particularly crunchy ones like broccoli. I planned to go back for a chocolate ice cream sandwich, maybe two of them.

Erika, whose two home refrigerators and freezer could, literally, feed a large party, settled for a melted cheese sandwich and a cappuccino from the new coffee maker which the cafeteria had recently gotten.

Maureen selected what Erika did. Maybe she's identifying with her, I thought, adding that she couldn't make a better choice.

A few minutes after we began eating, I started telling the story about Randy's experiment. Upon hearing the words "electric shock," Maureen let out another or her piercing screams. It was brief but afterward she seemed to lose her appetite and didn't touch her food again. And just like the last time a patient had screamed, all conversation in the cafeteria stopped but then was quickly resumed. I stopped telling my story and for the rest of the afternoon Maureen was her usual babyish self.

While Abram drove us back to Erika's house, she and I tried to make sense of what happened.

"Put it together and what do you get?" Erika

asked. "A girl who says only one word, room, and who freaks out when hearing about electric shock."

I didn't know, but Erika always thought more quickly than me.

"That she was tortured with electricity in a room. Or that she had seen it done to someone while being in that room."

Though driving, Abram seemed to have been listening to us closely.

"Maybe I can explain her behavior," he said.

Chapter 15

"Maureen was shocked," Abram said, from the front seat of the armored SUV.

"She sure was," I said. "Giving birth, the death of her parents. I can't imagine going through more." Though I was sure of what Erika imagined every day: being raped and murdered like her mother and sister.

"No, I mean shocked with electricity," Abram said in an annoyed tone. "Tortured, or seeing it being done."

What more could happen today, I thought. Now I was to hear another terrifying story.

"A year before I left my Vympel Unit (Erika later told me that this is an elite Russian Special Forces group) I was doing reconnaissance in southern Russia.

"The terrorists hated all Russians and particularly us. We had killed many of them quietly, and snipers are the most hated of all soldiers. You can't see them. They may be a quarter mile away in the brush. You're eating or walking to the latrine—until suddenly you aren't. You're lying dead on the ground because of a bullet that came from apparently nowhere. There's nothing more terrifying.

"So when they are captured, snipers aren't

allowed to die slowly. They used electricity on me to cause me pain, not to get information. We used it too. We also had fools.

"The best way to get information is not through physical pain but with psychological torture, which can leave deep mental scars even if the person was barely touched.

"First you try to strip away the prisoner's sense of self. You keep them naked and isolated in a windowless cell with artificial light which stays on all the time. You force them to be in uncomfortable positions for long periods so that their pain is internal and they don't blame you for it as they would if it came from beatings.

"Then they become dependent on you and seek your approval. The Stockholm Syndrome, it's called. You might slam a heavy door to emphasize to the prisoner that they are cut off from the rest of the world and have only you to rely on. This increases their need to think of you as a friend.

"I think that this is what happened to Maureen, and why the government is involved. Her parents and she were tortured for information using, or threatening to use, electricity."

"How did you manage to escape?" Erika asked, interrupting him.

Abram waited until the car was stopped at a red light before he replied. He looked at her in the rear view mirror as he spoke.

"I cut the cord which tied my hands on the jagged edge of a filing cabinet. When a guard came in with my food I killed him. Then I killed three others. When I got back to my unit we went back and killed the rest of them."

"How many were there?" I asked.

"There were twenty-three. Some weren't much older than you."

Usually we sat in front with Abram but today we were sitting in back While I had nothing to say, for middle school doesn't exactly prepare you for such stories, Erika did. She leaned forward and touched his shoulder. "I'm glad that you killed them," she said.

I studied her young face. Erika would be fourteen in thirty-six days but she was glad that Abram had killed the terrorists, even those boys who weren't much older than her.

Chapter 16

I had promised Randy that I would be home early that day but I felt too worn out to move. The alert at Erika's house and, most of all, the stories that I heard were simply too much. I felt as if I were living in a war movie: waiting to be shot at, waiting to shoot back, waiting to kill or to be killed.

Maybe I *should be* with Randy for he was the one who was great at killing the zombies in his video game, though the ones in his latest, *Dead Island*, wore bikinis. Maybe that was a step in my direction, or what he hoped it would be.

Gentle, kind Randy, the boy who was so frightened by the sight of blood that it made him want to vomit, spending his spare time, sometimes even when with me, using space age weapons to kill assorted creatures. Guns like those I saw earlier that day.

Erika was tired too. I had always envied her energy for no girl was involved in more activities than she. Though it wore me out just to hear about them, today had affected her too.

"Did you know that Taylor fights for love? That when he really wants a girl he goes after her and that in elementary school he competed against five boys for the attention of a girl he had a crush on. He didn't admit in *Twist* whether he won her but he did tell his guilty secret: that he hasn't missed an episode of *American Idol* in eight or nine years!"

Erika was the sturdiest person I knew, girl or boy, but I realized then that she was starting to lose it. She *never* had any interest in ordinary teenage craziness and was as likely to be interested in the contents of *Twist* as she would be to shear sheep for the 4H at the Connecticut Fair. Though if her father was thinking of buying *Twist* or if shearing a sheep would help persuade his business prospect to do something, she would willingly do both. So her comment about Taylor, a subject of no usual interest to her, meant that she was starting to lose it. Just as my other friends, Randy and Hillary and Brian, and me too, got a little crazy at times.

So I did what I do with them and what my older sister and Aunt Lena did with me: I listened without criticizing and felt that when the person sensed my caring they would calm down and they usually did.

Sometimes, with Randy, I also implied that if he came over my house he would get from me what his fantasies told him that he wanted though he wound up settling for a back rub. That year neither of us was really ready for sex so just kissing and holding each other was all I let him do. After a few minutes of my just being there for her, Erika started doing what naturally calmed her.

When boys are stressed out they often play video games, but many girls cook. Erika, like my older sister, was into cooking. Both found the ritual of finding the recipe and then measuring and folding or cutting the ingredients to be soothing.

Unlike me, both Erika and my sister are great cooks. Where they got their talent from I have no idea since my mother is a terrible cook and Erika's mother, having been a doctor with a live-in cook, did little except to pass the plates. But Erika was a great baker, and that afternoon's project was her famous brownies.

These were the only baked goods which were worth the price, and far more, at the library's bake sale which was held twice a year. She was offered a summer intern job at two local restaurants but turned the offers down. Cooking relaxed her: it would never be her job.

So being my usual klutzy self, I only followed her orders and offered to wash the dishes though, considering the industrial sized dishwasher in her home, this wouldn't be needed. I sat and listened as she described exactly what she was doing. She didn't seem to be able to stop talking and I realized that she was more tense than me and trying to calm herself through her cooking routine.

This made sense to me since when I am nervous I often repeated something. I never understood why until Erika explained it by telling me what her psychologist had told her about herself. That doing a simple activity, like cleaning or cooking, is a natural way that the mind helps one to relax.

Erika didn't often talk about her therapy since her doctor told her not to. He said that if she did then she would soon hesitate to tell him anything. I wasn't sure about this but it seemed to make sense to Erika so I wasn't about to object. Her father was paying her doctor a lot more money than I would ever earn for less than an hour's work. So, like I said, I just listened and tried not to interrupt her.

"Never use 'dutched cocoa'! The cocoa powder I use is made from roasted cocoa beans which are ground to a paste and pressed to remove most of the fat, then ground into a powder. If you 'dutch' it, to make it less acidic, it looks darker than natural cocoa powder so you might think that it is better but it doesn't taste as chocolaty. I'll read off the ingredients and you measure them."

I didn't like being treated as another of her hired help but, like I said, Erika was feeling badly and she was one of my two best friends. Though Randy is the love of my life, boys as friends don't count. Though I expected that he would always stick by me, even this young girl knew that while you can count on your girlfriend for a lifetime, who could really be sure how long a boy would stay around whether you wound up marrying him or not.

So while Erika sprawled on one of the well-padded kitchen chairs and sipped her iced cappuccino, I followed her orders which included getting the ingredients, and doing the measurements. First, I found the nonstick vegetable oil spray. Then I cut one and a quarter sticks of butter into one inch pieces, followed by measuring one and a quarter cups of sugar, three-quarters cup of cocoa, a teaspoon of vanilla extract, two eggs, one-half cup of all-purpose flour, and a cup of walnut pieces. Getting these wasn't as bad as it might seem since the walnuts were already shelled so all I had to do was to measure them.

This was the easy part. Then I had to line the baking pan with foil and coat it with the nonstick spray, melt the butter while continuing to stir it, then removing it from the heat and adding in and stirring the sugar, cocoa, and vanilla. After letting this mixture cool, I blended in the eggs and, finally, added in the flour and then the nuts.

Erika counted while I beat it sixty times. The baking took twenty-five minutes in a three hundred twenty-five degree oven. While it cooled, I poured myself a glass of orange juice and sprawled in a chair opposite Erika.

Baking these brownies worked and Erika looked her normal self even before we began eating them. They were great. Maybe, I thought, if I developed the interest and followed directions even I could become a good cook.

OK, maybe the brownies weren't as good as Nabisco's Mallomar cookies which I love and are, I consider, the best cookie in America. But in a contest at my school, it would be a toss-up between them.

Once Erika became her usual calm self, she became quiet and her thinking seemed back on track.

"About Maureen..." she said.

"Yes?"

"Why do you think that your Aunt Lena asked you to help her?"

"It was as a favor to me, to us. We were going crazy hanging around all summer doing nothing."

"You really think it was that?"

"Yes, don't you?"

Erika didn't say anything for a few moments. She looked towards the tray of brownies which were cooling on the table.

"No."

"What then?"

"My dad and your Aunt Lena have become friendly..."

About which I was glad for, like I said, they would make a great couple. Both were rich and super-bright and could have beautiful children together. But I didn't say this. Erika wasn't ready to hear it so soon after her mother's death.

"So?"

"Why did Maureen wind up in Greenwich? It's a tiny town when she could have been sent to a huge medical center in New York City or Chicago or San Francisco?"

"The government liked Rillston Hospital?"

"Did you know that they just got a contract to treat government employees. Those who work for the three letter agencies: FBI, CIA, NSA. There was a scandal two months ago after it was found out that the hospital they had been using gave patients electric shock treatment and was experimenting with lobotomies. That's where they cut out parts of the brain."

I was horrified, and joked, "That might improve government intelligence services. Maybe avoid another World Trade Center bombing."

Erika smiled to show that she agreed, but just for a moment.

I wondered why Erika was questioning me. It was as if she was laying out pieces of a puzzle and wanting me to put them together. Just like with those government employees who deal with secrets, or detectives when they are trying to solve a mystery. Why didn't she just tell me? Or did the whole matter make her so uncomfortable that she could only speak of it a little at a time.

"What do you think of Maureen?"

"She's beautiful. Eurasian, isn't she?"

"Yes. Her mother, as a teenager, was a famous Chinese model. When she grew too old to model she studied at the University of Chicago and became a physicist."

"How do you know?" I was puzzled for Dr. Bradley had told us nothing about Maureen's background."

"Though I never met him, her father was my

uncle. Maureen is my cousin."

Chapter 17

Talk about trust! I loved Aunt Lena and knew that she loved me. She was even my godmother. Still, both she and Dr. Bradley appeared to have lied both to me and Erika. Maybe not lied directly, but certainly not told us the whole truth.

Dr. Bradley said that nothing was known about Maureen's background. Or did he? Hadn't he really said that they knew nothing about what happened to her before she was brought to Rillston Hospital and I then drew my own conclusion from this, which turned out to be wrong.

Maureen did benefit from me and Erika trying to be her friend. So Aunt Lena's statement that Maureen needed us had been true. Could the suggestion of our volunteering have come originally from Erika's father when they met? He knew my Aunt Lena and was thinking of investing in a health management consulting firm which she was starting.

But did Aunt Lena know that Maureen was Erika's cousin? And why didn't Erika tell me this before we met Maureen? If you want to know something you ask, my lawyer-father always said, so I did. I hoped to get the truth since we were both drugged on the absolutely wonderful brownies that I (OK, with Erika's instructions) had baked.

"Why didn't you tell me that you and Maureen were cousins?"

Erika took a bite of her brownie before answering. Then she opened her mouth and took another. Then she slowly wiped her lips, which didn't need this attention, with a napkin.

"I didn't know what to say. I never met her or her parents. My father, for much the same unknown reason that your parents avoid your Aunt Lena, considered my uncle to be the family's black sheep and never spoke of him. Every family has secrets and I only know those which I've told you. Just you know what happened to my mother and sister and about 'Z.'"

I couldn't criticize Erika since I had my own big secret which I hadn't shared with her: my God husband, Babaluaiye. At that moment I felt envious of other soon-to-be eighth graders who were free to worry about the lives of Justin and Gregg and Rob and other substitutes for the real life lover they wanted. I had the same thoughts too, though not about them.

After my periods began I started putting on weight about my hips and breasts though one breast was still a little bigger than the other. I also had a dream about having sex with Randy, who I described in *Margaret of Greenwich* as lusting after my butt. Now there was even more for him to want!

I wondered what boy Erika hungered for, or if her passion was contained by the thought of the business empire she would one day inherit.

"You have a dreamy look on your face, like Hillary gets when she's thinking of her Bill," Erika said.

"I was thinking about Randy, and whether we would be able to hold off having sex until we're married."

"Why do you want to wait? What harm can having sex do? With all the time that you see him you're practically living together now."

"I know and I don't know. Maybe I'm afraid of getting pregnant."

"He can use a condom or I'll get the pill from my doctor. He's very accommodating. I'll say it's for me."

"What would your dad say?"

"He won't know. There's doctor-patient confidentiality and like I say: the doctor is very accommodating. Besides, my dad trusts me completely and considers my sex life as being only my business. He has much bigger things to worry about."

I considered. Maybe I should take Erika up on her offer. I was sure that she would let Randy and me use one of the many spare bedrooms in her house, for several hours or even several years if we wanted. Her dad liked kids and Randy would be a great audience for him. He might even turn out to be her dad's youngest employee!

But Randy and I weren't ready. Having sex, though it was scientifically as ordinary as eating, involved strong emotions: love, trust, and for me, commitment.

I considered Randy to be the love of my life but I was still only fourteen. Would he hold this place in my heart when I was fifteen or twenty-five or forty?

Because I couldn't answer this question, I avoided making a decision, dribbled the basketball like my sports minded friends would say.

"If you got the pill for me and I didn't start taking it now, how long would they remain effective?"

"They'll be OK nearly forever so long as it isn't very humid or hot and they're kept out of the light."

"OK. Buy them and I'll pay you back when I save the money."

"Forget about paying me! Someday I'll ask you for a favor. I'll get a prescription for a year's supply and a

Pillpak with a built-in alarm to remind you when to take it. I'll get you two dozen condoms too, in case you start worrying and want to be really sure. They'll keep for four years. You can store the stuff here and take it whenever you want."

"I hope that your dad doesn't find it."

"He better not go through my things!" Erika replied with a hint of anger.

I looked at her face and believed her. But I also wondered what else, if anything, she might be hiding.

We munched on more brownies and got back to our business.

Chapter 18

"What do you think is going on with Maureen?" I asked Erika. "I feel like we're worker ants being manipulated by the Queen Bee."

"I don't know. Let's look at the situation, how my dad does when he's deciding whether to buy a company. First look at the facts and then the people. What information do we have that we can rely on?"

"I'd trust what both Dr. Bradley and my Aunt Lena said. That Maureen gave birth but nothing was known about her child; that her parents were both dead and involved in some way with the American government; and that she had some terrible experience which blew her mind so she is now behaving like a baby. wanting to go back to being a child and to begin life all over again in order to repair her mind."

"I'll go along with that, and also what Abram said: that she may have been tortured with electricity or witnessed it being done to her parents."

"Why would they torture her?"

"To get information from her parents."

This made sense to me.

"Can we trust what Dr. Bradley said?" Erika

asked.

"He's an employee of the hospital and would have no reason to lie. Besides, he sounded pretty honest."

"You can't tell, older sister." I was only two months older than Erika but liked being called her sister. Maybe that's what good girlfriends are, I thought, or perhaps there was something more special between us.

"Aunt Lena?" she asked.

"She'd never deliberately lie to me. I'd stake my life on it," I replied, for I had.

"OK, but the hospital has a contract to treat government workers. Probably both she and Dr. Bradley are just doing their jobs and above board."

"So the government might be the Queen Bee," I said. "They know more than they're revealing and are using us worker bees to find out things. Maybe how much Maureen knows."

"Or how much she knows but doesn't realize that she knows, facts she picked up. And who better to share this with than girls her own age, during casual conversations while talking about boys and teachers. I think my dad knows more than he's told us."

"Why do you say that?"

"He's very smart and not one to be manipulated.

If we figured this out, then he must have too, and before Maureen arrived in Greenwich. He's probably working with the government. They'd trust him with anything.

"One of his companies makes defense electronics and he has a 'top secret restricted' security clearance. The only other people having that are those who design atomic weapons."

No wonder their house is a fortress, I thought, and another thought bothered me. If her father had access to such huge military secrets, why was their house guarded by Russians? I asked Erika this in a round-about way.

"Isn't the government afraid that their secrets might be seen by Abram or one of the other Russian bodyguards around?"

"My father is super cautious. They were first hired by the government when they arrived in this country. They are the best soldiers that Russia had and were given warm welcomes. Don't worry. You're safe being around them."

I did believe her, but also wondered how, if the Russians were such good bodyguards, her mother and sister wound up being murdered. But this question I didn't ask.

I got up, hugged her, and grabbed my backpack.

Margaret and Erika

After all that happened that day, I just wanted to be home.

Chapter 19

Home is where the heart is, I thought, and where they must take you in as a poet once wrote. When I arrived home I was sleepy from eating too many brownies but also worried.

I always got at least two phone calls a day from Randy. On days when he was really nervous I got many more. That's what girlfriends are for, right?

But today there had been none. Either he had stopped being such a worrier, which I doubted, or he found another girlfriend. One who was more open than me and not just with her heart. Maybe she had a nicer butt, which Randy seemed obsessed with, and bigger boobs too.

"Things seem better after a nap," my dad had always advised, and I followed his advice that evening. I took off my sneakers and, without undressing further, threw myself on my bed. Within moments I was asleep.

You would have thought that after my talk with Erika that day about birth control and my fantasy of having sex with Randy that my dream would have involved having sex with him. But it didn't. Instead, Erika and Maureen and I were naked and chained to the wall of a cell without windows. The light in the ceiling was so bright that every physical blemish on us could be clearly seen. Erika and Maureen didn't have any.

I wondered if I didn't look like one big pimple for the tiny one on my cheek had started to worry me. I heard the creaking sound from the heavy steel door as it began opening. Three men in white coats then entered the room. One wheeled a hospital cart with all types of torture equipment on it: a blowtorch, a box with clamps leading from it, small knives and pliers.

The men focused on Maureen first. They attached the clamps to her nipples and asked her a question which I couldn't make out. When she didn't answer one of the men turned the dial of the small box on the cart. I saw the clamps on her nipples begin to turn red and was awakened by the sound of Maureen's screams.

The dream had seemed so real that the moment I awoke I thought that I was back in the cell and awaiting my turn to be tortured. Then I recognized my room: my desk with the stuffed animals, my bookcase with my mother's old Nancy Drew mystery novels, the photo of me and Randy.

It was just a dream, I told myself. They're not real and nothing to be afraid of. Dreams are your friends, Erika's psychologist had told her. They tell you how you see your life and what is bothering you. "Can they predict the future?" Erika had asked him. "Only when there is something which worries you, like when you dream that a very sick relative dies. If they do, you may think that your dream predicted their death though it only meant that you were worried about them.

"Or if there are similar things in your dream to what you later see, like a particular car or street scene, you may think that you predicted it. But this is called *deja vu* and was long understood by psychologists. It means that both experiences had *similar* elements."

What he said made sense to me when Erika told me, and still did. But a lingering thought remained. That Erika and I and maybe Maureen too were in danger though Erika seemed the likely major target. The dream might have predicted my general worry about this. But could it have predicted our future too? This was not a pleasant thought, particularly in the quiet, rich town of Greenwich, Connecticut.

It was eight twenty-five and Randy still hadn't called. My mother had let me sleep through dinner. I warmed the food she left for me in the microwave and, after I ate, went to ask my older sister, Melody, for advice. She would be a senior when school started and, being so much older, had provided me with good advice about boys in the past. My relationship with Randy had always been a high maintenance one!

I told her my worry, which she downplayed.

"Stop worrying. You just turned fourteen. You'll have lots of boyfriends."

"Maybe." I was already spending too much time studying myself in the mirror and usually didn't like what I saw.

"You *will*," she insisted. "You're smart and pretty and any guy that doesn't love you at first sight isn't worth much so you're better off without him."

When she said this I wanted to hug her but didn't. Melody wasn't a hugger.

So I just listened and began to glow with her compliments and realized that maybe that was what I had really been seeking. Not advice about boys but compliments to make me feel better. Melody could always be counted on for these.

"Why not call him and see what's going on. You don't have to wait for him to call. This is the twenty-first century. The old rule that it was the guys who asked for the date is dying but not yet dead so it's understandable why you feel uncomfortable calling him.

"It might also be that you're afraid to be rejected though this is a big fear of boys too. It's so great that many boys don't date. They're terrified of how they will feel if they are turned down. With some boys their first date winds up being with the girl they marry no matter how good or bad a match it is. *Call him.* What's the risk? That you'll have to find a new boyfriend tomorrow, something which I'm sure you'll be able to do. Not every boy in Greenwich is a total idiot."

After hearing this can you wonder why I consider Melody to be the best sister in the world? Wouldn't you want her? And wouldn't any boy want to marry her, I thought, though this event did worry me: I didn't want to lose her. Not for a long time at least.

As usual, I followed my sister's advice but waited until nine-fifteen when I decided that he must be home. Randy was, and he picked up on the second ring.

My first impulse was to yell at him but I didn't. Instead, I behaved as would a long suffering but continuously attentive wife.

"How *are* you. I was worried when you didn't call."

"I'm sorry, sorry, sorry," he almost cried, and I immediately felt better. There was no other girl with a better butt and boobs. It was still me. But something must have happened.

"What is it?" I asked.

"You'll never believe it. I still can't."

"Well, what?" I repeated, now allowing myself some exasperation in my voice.

"My mom was feeling sick and we just got back from the Emergency Room."

"How is she?"

"She's fine but my dad and I are feeling crazy."

Why do boys talk so indirectly? No wonder the world is in such a mess. With effort, I managed to control myself.

"OK," I said calmly. "Now just tell me what happened."

"My dad can hardly believe it. I can't yet believe it even though the doctor is sure."

This is the boy I plan to marry? I asked myself and tried again.

"What can't you believe?"

"My mom is having a baby."

Chapter 20

A baby, I thought. First, Maureen gave birth, then Erika agrees to stash the pill and condoms for me, and now the news of Randy's mother being pregnant. The world seemed awash in pregnant women and I hoped that I wouldn't be next.

"How old is your mom?"

"Forty-one, though she tells people that she's thirty-six."

That's what happens when you get older, I thought, lies creep in. But back to the main business: keeping Randy calm and focused on the big picture which was his career, our marriage, and someday, before I was older than his mother, our children.

"Do they know what it will be?"

"Not yet. My mom is hoping for a girl."

That's understandable, I thought. Just a few months before, when dealing with the problems which I had involved Randy in, his parents had seemed ready to put him up for adoption.

I wondered how Randy would cope with having a baby sister or brother and becoming a second class citizen in his family. It wasn't like that in my family but the age difference between the children, four years, wasn't that great. The nearly fifteen years between Randy and the baby would be a huge gulf . Would he play with the child or ignore him/her? Might he be jealous at the attention the baby received and hit the child? I knew this could happen but I doubted that gentle Randy would behave like that. And if he did then he would get twice back from me and my friend Emily, who was a martial arts expert.

But why was I even considering this? Randy had never hit anyone in his life and the only trouble he ever got into was done innocently or from trying to help another person. He was as close to being as angelic a son as parents could get, and was brilliant to boot. And, though he blushed when anyone said it, he was growing into a fantastic looking boy.

I know that saying this might me sound as air-headed as Hillary does when she fantasizes about former President Clinton. But I would love Randy no matter what though isn't it pleasanter to have a good looking face to look at?

About his body I can't say, since I've never seen it. He's not into swimming or laying around a pool so the most that I have seen is when he wears shorts during the summer and it certainly looks OK.

He's not fat or real skinny and considering that his father is a doctor I'm sure that he eats well and is healthy. At least he mostly does when he is around me since I make sure of that.

This may make me sound bossy which is not a nice thing to be. But isn't every good girlfriend and wife bossy, for this just means, in my mind, being watchful enough that their man remains healthy. Can you criticize me for this? Shouldn't every girlfriend behave the same?

If a girl isn't willing to take care of her man then what use is she to him? Yes, certainly for sex, but for a relationship to last, more than that is needed especially since my cooking is barely passable. I'll never be a great cook like my older sister or Erika. But I will care for Randy like no other girl can and this is why we'll both be the only love for each other.

So I returned to another of my major duties: taking care of Randy.

"How do you feel about having a baby in your family?"

"Besides me, you mean?" he asked.

I was glad that Randy was developing a sense of humor. Mine tended to be weird and having to explain your jokes is no laughing matter, to make another of my small puns.

"Besides you," I agreed, though in a playful and not sarcastic tone.

"It would be new for me. I've never been around a baby. I'll have a lot of things to learn, like how to talk to a baby and play with them."

Now he needs my support, I told myself. "You'll be a great older brother," I said with a reassuring tone, though I felt that it would be years before he would be a good recruit for mine and Erika's babysitting business.

"When is the baby due?"

"I don't know. I didn't ask."

I returned to my other worry. "I need to talk to you. Not about us but about volunteer work which Erika and I are doing at Rillston Hospital. Can you come over now and maybe stay over?"

"I probably can. I'll tell my parents that I want you and Melody to teach me how to cope with a baby. Besides, they're so excited they hardly notice me."

"I'm sure that's not true," I said, still being supportive. "I'll keep the light on for you, like it says in the hotel ad." But not the one in my bedroom, I told myself, not tonight.

Chapter 21

Randy came but he couldn't sleep over. He wanted to, or so he said, but his mother wouldn't let him no matter how persuasive he was, he insisted. I gave him a smile but I wasn't convinced. Did he try hard enough? Had the news of his new family addition so blown his mind that he was looking for another girlfriend? One who was readier to have sex than me?

Aunt Lena said that sex keeps boyfriends coming around. But not for you, she would then add. Yet why not for me? Hadn't menstruating made me a fully capable woman? One who should decide for herself how her body should be used?

Erika was still a virgin but she certainly thought so. Her status had nothing to do with uncertainty about having sex but the difficulty of finding a boy to have it with. He had to come from a family nearly as wealthy as hers, and be someone who wouldn't be frightened off by her armed bodyguards hovering about.

Hillary had lost her virginity (this is a dumb phrase isn't it? as if it was something which could be found) even before her menstruation began, and to her seventeen-year-old cousin too!

What was it with me?

I dropped these troubling thoughts from my mind and made hot chocolate for Randy, adding to his snack several of the brownies from Erika's house. I was saving them for my sisters but Randy needed them more. If he was bored with me they would impress him! And I did bake them, even if it was just by following Erika's instructions.

But Randy didn't seem like he was bored with me. I concluded that by noting that he still stared at my butt and tried to score points as we sat together on the sofa, which I let him do. After all, he was my boyfriend and they do have some rights. So I let him massage my breasts until the nipples rose and I began to have a strange feeling which is hard to describe. Then I took his hand away but kissed him too so he didn't feel rejected.

I began thinking. For the past few months Randy had been satisfied with hand-holding and a kiss. Then it was the squeeze of my breast against his shoulder while I rubbed his neck or patted his back. Now he was rubbing my breasts. What would satisfy him next, I wondered or was that even the right question to ask. Wasn't it up to me to set the limits on how far we go?

Would it be wise for me to start on the pill now, or stash condoms in my backpack?

It was a good time to get Randy thinking about something else.

"I have a problem," I said.

"So do I," he moaned, as he reached for me. My Randy was getting randy, as they say.

"OK, OK," I said firmly. "Tonight is not the night for me to get pregnant. I need your help with something serious."

"This *is* serious," he insisted.

What happened to Randy? He was never this pushy before. I had been the one to push kisses on him. Maybe it was the news of his new brother or sister which changed him by forcing him out of the child role in his family which he had been playing.

I pushed him away again, but gently. I wanted to leave him with the hope of future success which, as my very experienced Aunt Lena advised, would keep him coming back.

"I want you too, now and forever, but not tonight," I whispered. Then I threw my arms about his neck and kissed him hard, forcing my tongue into his mouth. Don't ask me where I learned this for I was operating by trial-and-error and hoped that he wouldn't bite my tongue out of shock.

Thankfully, he didn't. His mouth tasted of

chocolate and I can't say that I particularly enjoyed this experience though he obviously did. A moment later he was on top of me. Seconds later we heard my mother walking down the stairs to the rec room where we lay sprawled on the sofa.

I have quick reactions and, still being bigger than Randy, I quickly shoved him onto the other side of the sofa and grabbed the cup of cocoa. By the time my mother reached the basement floor, we were seated side-by-side and Randy was pointing at something in the latest issue of *Gamepro* which he always carried. We probably looked innocent to my mother though I did wonder if she noticed Randy's red face and our heavy breathing.

"Ten more minutes, children," she remarked, before returning upstairs.

"I need your advice," I said to Randy, as the sound of my mother's steps faded. I held him stiffly so he wouldn't try another move on me. I made a memo to myself to educate him about the difference between persistence, which is valued by a girl, and rape, which is not.

"Erika and I have been volunteering at Rillston Hospital. We're trying to help a fourteen-year-old girl who went through a terrible time. Both of her parents were murdered, and she gave birth though we don't know what happened to her child. She behaves like our baby sister when we are around. Waiting for us to suggest an activity and then going along with it whatever it is. She hardly ever talks and when she does she only repeats the word 'room.'

"We've been trying to speak with her about typical teen stuff so I told her about your experiments with electricity. When I said the words 'electric shock' she freaked out and screamed.

"Abram, one of Erika's bodyguards, thinks that she might have been tortured with electric shock, which usually doesn't leave marks. Or that she saw her parents or someone else being tortured with it. Also, the government is paying for her treatment so something big might have been involved."

I could feel Randy's body relax as I spoke. He was getting interested in this new problem and no longer strained against my grip which was keeping his hands from slipping under my shirt.

"Does she do anything else which seems strange?" he asked.

"When we color in coloring books..."

"Color?" he asked in a condescending tone.

"Not that we want to but it seemed like Maureen

would enjoy it since she acts like a baby. And she does, but she doesn't color. All she does is to write a letter and some numbers. I have them here." I reached into my pocket and took out the note. "W88, 2, 172, 1522."

Randy's hand dropped to his side and he looked startled "What...what...what else do you know about her?" Randy stutters when he's nervous.

"We know absolutely nothing. She's Erika's cousin though you wouldn't think so even if both are stunningly beautiful. She's Eurasian. Her mother was Chinese."

Randy didn't say anything for a few seconds. He was so quiet that I wondered if he would say anything. What he did surprised me even more.

His arms relaxed and he moved away from me, as if I were radioactive or that my body held a virus he could catch.

"Haven't you gotten me into enough trouble?" he asked angrily, and I wondered if this would be our first real argument. If so, it would be a big one for his face turned red and having sex with me now seemed the last thing on his mind.

But, being his girlfriend (we are made to suffer, aren't we?) I didn't respond in kind. I just reached for his hand and asked, sweetly, "What do you mean?" though I knew what he meant. Months before, while trying to help my friend, Laurie, I had gotten Randy involved in two break-ins and computer hacking. We were both nearly murdered too. But, like my dad who is a very good lawyer once said, "If you have the evidence on your side you talk evidence but if your client is guilty then you must deny, deny, deny!"

The innocent look which I kept on my face was intended as my denial.

"Randy, you're being upset for no reason. Maureen can't hurt you. She's just a fourteen-year-old girl like me."

"Laurie was thirteen and look what happened when we tried helping her. Do you have any idea what you're involved in?"

I didn't. "No. And that's why Erika and I need your help. You are the smartest boy we know, and soon you'll be taller than me." Like Aunt Lena says, when in trouble, pile on the compliments. She also suggested to change the subject, but the subject which so upset him was why I needed his help. Still, he did calm down.

"OK, OK. I'm sorry I got so angry."

"Well you should be," I murmured and moved closer, putting my arm around his shoulder and leaning against him. I kissed his neck and murmured, "My man." It was a good line and move and worked though I couldn't remember what movie I got it from.

"It's just...just...that what you're dealing with is...deep shit."

What he said shocked me. Not the words for I had heard them before and used them (rarely) in conversation with my older sister. But that Randy had spoken them. Randy had never talked like that, at least not to me. Still, he tried to express himself gently and kissed me back before repeating himself.

"You're in the deepest shit."

Chapter 22

Randy explained what he thought was going on. Slowly, so that I understood. Though I am smart and got an "A" in Science, that class mostly involved biology which interested me. But what Randy talked about was atomic physics, a subject which isn't taught in any high school and certainly not in any middle school. Like I said, Randy is a genius.

When he finished talking, if he was right, then what we tried to do months before, getting Laurie out of her affair with her art teacher, was nothing compared to what we were dealing with now.

It was, as Randy had put it, "deep shit."

Randy reads a lot. Some is the Harry Potter stuff which he loves but I can't get involved in no matter how much he encourages me. I have enough troubles to worry about and don't need made-up ones.

But Randy also reads a lot about real-life events, and particularly the lives of scientists. This makes sense since he wants to be one. And, hopefully, a scientist with a job so he doesn't become another of the many unemployed we read about. Those staying at home to care for the kids while their wives work and earn the lower salary than men which women still get.

This is starting to sound like a political speech so I'll get back to what Randy told me, and in his own words.

"The 'W88' which Maureen wrote down relates to the W-88 atomic bomb warhead on the Trident nuclear submarine, each of which carries twenty-four of these missiles.

"Each nuclear warhead is a MIRV which means 'multiply targeted re-entry independent vehicle.' Each missile carries several atomic bombs which are intended for different targets and are released by the missile as they come into target range.

"The sizes of the original atomic bombs which totally destroyed Hiroshima and Nagasaki during World War Two was huge. A B-29 Super Fortress bomber carrying just one of them could barely lift off the runway. The W-88 warheads are tiny in comparison. That's how several can fit on each Trident missile.

"The other numbers which Maureen wrote, '2' and '172' and '1522,' are technical details of the missile. Do you understand what I've said so far?"

Randy was now talking to me just like Mr. Reilly, who was the best science teacher I ever had. Randy was also behaving more like a grown-up than he usually did.

"So far it's clear," I replied, and he continued.

"OK. Atomic bombs consist of two parts. A core which is called 'the primary' made up of plutonium-239 or highly enriched uranium, which is the size of a grapefruit; and ordinary explosives which compress it and create the chain reaction.

"This sets off a secondary, more powerful fusion bomb. It's called a 'fusion bomb' because when it goes off, deuterium and tritium fuse, which is similar to what happens within the sun.

"The '2' refers to the two points at which the explosives are placed, rather than surrounding the entire core. The numbers '172' and '1522' refer to the 172mm radius of the secondary, just under seven inches; and the 1522mm, or just over five feet, is the length of the warhead.

"This was top-secret stuff until government investigations revealed it. But the biggest secret of all was never discovered and they're probably still looking."

"Who is looking?"

"Every FBI and CIA agent who wants to be top-dog."

Now I was getting frustrated. Randy can make science understandable to just about anyone but the need to present basic facts seems to always escape him.

"OK, now in a few words, exactly what are these people looking for?"

Randy smiled at me. He actually smiled. The same look I get from lousy teachers when I ask a question which they consider dumb. But he seemed to notice that I was getting angry for the smile quickly left his face.

"I'm sorry," he apologized. "What all these government agents want to know is the identity of the spy who gave these secrets to China. Like I said, you two girls are into deep shit."

Chapter 23

Wow, double wow, I thought. I spend my afternoon with Erika talking about the pill and condoms in the unlikely event that I decide to have sex with Randy and then he throws this at me. Telling me that Erika and I are involved with atomic secrets and spies and the CIA. But I quickly calmed down.

Randy hadn't done anything except be a good friend and help us to understand what we were really dealing with. And as my dad always said, information is power. So we were certainly in a better situation now than a few hours before when we were walking around blindfolded, so to speak.

Then, maybe because I had been so angry with Randy this time when he didn't deserve it, I kissed him again. A long hard one before pulling away and going upstairs quickly, for I felt uneasy.

The limits of what I was allowing Randy seemed to be changing and I now wasn't sure where they were. I reminded myself that Erika hadn't yet bought the condoms for me and that I didn't want to wind up like Maureen though I was sure that far more than giving birth had caused her craziness.

Margaret and Erika

Still, exactly what were me and Erika doing? Not chasing a spy but just trying to be a good friend to a girl who had none. What harm could come from that? I couldn't see any. If what we were doing was dangerous then certainly Aunt Lena, who owned and ran Rillston Hospital and was my godmother too, would have stopped us. But only if she knew what we now know, I concluded.

True, judging by what Maureen had done so far: piercing screams, repeatedly speaking one word and scribbling assorted numbers, we knew nothing which could harm anyone. That is *unless* someone believed otherwise, *unless* Maureen started speaking, *unless, unless, unless.*

But I couldn't live a life like this, I told myself, worrying about every little thing that might happen. 'Z,' the murdering enemy of Erika and her father, was a real threat. Maureen was just an interesting puzzle for me and Erika and Randy to solve.

She was only a girl our age who we wanted to help. But look what happened the last time I tried being helpful, as Sergeant Alamo had proudly described at my fourteenth birthday party: I had "helped my friends, my town, and my government." He left out that I almost got killed doing these things.

My giving more such help and Greenwich would erect a statue of me to place alongside the others in the town park: *For Margaret, the dumbest fourteen-year-old who lived in Greenwich since it was founded in sixteen-forty.*

Still, I was now at home with my loving family, safe behind a locked door and protected by my father with his pistol. I might also be protected, if He approved of my behavior, by my husband, the Orisha God Babaluaiye.

I felt depressed and knew that I needed to talk to my dad for I always felt better afterward.

Since my dad developed Lyme disease he no longer went to his office. This, he had told me, would have driven him crazy if he didn't have a profession he could follow at home. So he now spent his days writing articles for law journals, to keep himself busy and his name in the public eye until he re-opened his practice. This was his hope and that of our family too. We ached for him, far less because of the poverty which the loss of his income had caused us.

What actually had I lost, I asked myself. We ate better than most people thanks to help from the government's food stamp program and the Mormon food bank. And no students cared if my clothes, as was obvious, came from the Salvation Army store in Port Chester. One of my two best girlfriends, Erika, the only child of the town's billionaire, certainly didn't, and she was kind enough to dress down whenever we met.

But being poor had caused stress in our family. We no longer had Internet access at home so to get on the Internet we had to go to the library, and our phones were now pre-paid and only for use in an emergency. No smart phones for us!

Things were hardest on my mother who had to cope with the bills. My dad's monthly Social Security Disability check wasn't that much for a family of five and having to decide how to spend ten dollars, which is chump change for teenagers in the rich town of Greenwich, required serious decision making. Should my mother buy two and a half gallons of gas for our twelve year old car, or twelve cans of the cheapest tuna, or the large bottle of multivitamins which was on sale. These were daily decisions having to be made by a woman who was naturally nervous.

When you were used to living on my dad's earlier income, which was a bit under three hundred thousand dollars a year (our parents don't believe in keeping such things secret from their children), suddenly losing nine-tenths of it takes a big adjustment.

What we children learned is that having a parent unemployed is a family experience. No matter how much your parents try to protect you from the reality of it, everyone changes. They worry where every penny goes and try to control everything, being afraid that some new emergency will throw the budget out of whack.

You find yourself getting angry about nothing, and also becoming sad and depressed. To sum it up in a few words, being poor isn't fun.

My dad didn't look like he was having fun either. When I went to his home office he was seated in his favorite La-Z-Boy rocker but was looking out the window at apparently nothing. Usually he would be typing away on his computer or reading the law journal articles which I had gotten for him from the library.

I would e-mail them to Randy or Erika and they would print them out for me. The library charged ten cents a page and the hundreds of pages which I got for my dad would have seriously wrecked the family budget.

Looking at the sad look on my dad's face, I tried to think of how I might cheer him up. Managing to keep cheerful is a big job when you're poor.

He waved me over and smiled. I squeezed into the chair alongside him. It was a big squeeze but neither of us minded. Since my menstruation began I had been "hippy."

"How is my little girl?" he asked. He called all of his daughters "little girl," even my seventeen-year-old sister.

"I'm OK. How are you?"

Usually when I asked this, my dad would reply "fine" or "great" and give me a cheery smile, one like presidents give in their news photos. This time he didn't. Maybe he's starting to see me as being more of a grown-up I thought. Or my having nearly been murdered had changed the way he was relating to me. Wanting us to have real sharing and not just behave like fathers and daughters are supposed to act.

What my dad then said surprised me. For the first time ever the sad look which I noticed on his face stayed, and he talked about himself rather than questioning me.

"I get down at times, like all people in my position. Being sick is bad enough but not being able to give you and your mother the kind of life you should have is much worse.

"We have the kind of life we want," I said. "Any life we have with you is just fine."

Dad then kissed me on the forehead, for he knew I

was trying to cheer him up.

"I hope to get back to the office. I can't explain exactly why but I am feeling better. Maybe it's from being off the antibiotic, which heals but also screws up your insides. My new doctor recommended self-hypnosis and she gave me a self-hypnotic relaxation CD. Did you know that some doctors use hypnosis to get rid of warts?"

"You're kidding."

"No. Warts are caused by a virus which the body's natural immune system has the power to kill. If you have just a small wart the dermatologist will freeze it off but if the warts are over a large part of your body they can't do this so they use hypnosis. It's very relaxing. You can use it too. I've tried to get your mother to use it but I wasn't successful. She said that listening to the CD made her nervous.

"When I asked the doctor about this she said that your mother's reaction sometimes happened with people who are very nervous. The calming reaction which hypnosis produces is so new and strange an experience that they begin feeling even more nervous. But this would go away if the person continued using it, which I'm encouraging her to do."

My dad really is starting to see me as a grown-up,

I thought. Never before had he spoken so openly about my mother. I tried opening this door a bit more.

"How does it feel not being a lawyer like you were?"

"I still *am* a lawyer. I just no longer have an office or clients," he said with a smile. "But to answer your question more honestly: I miss it. Not just the income though that certainly is important, but the feeling of being involved in the world, of having an impact on it. Being involved with the people who relied on me for doing a good job, and the satisfaction I got from doing it. I enjoyed answering their questions, providing advice, and being important in their lives."

"You're important in our life," I said, and dad hugged me and kissed my forehead again.

"Understand that when I am angry it's not because of what you or anyone in our family did. It's just the normal feeling which an unemployed person can get from being on a daily emotional roller coaster.

"You'll only make me angry if you ever betray your principles and let yourself down. Though I never expect for this to happen, you'll always be my daughter."

I didn't reply for what could I say? That he was the best father in the world. I changed the subject.

"Dad, can I ask you a legal question?"

"Of course you can. Is Randy in trouble again?" Dad was referring to the scrape he had helped Randy out of during the past school year.

"No, everything is fine with him. I just have a simple question. If Erika and I discover a really big government secret, can we get into trouble?"

Chapter 24

My dad just looked at me. He didn't push me away as if I was radioactive as Randy had done though his look seemed to ask, "What trouble have you gotten into now?" So I told him. But not about the death threat towards Erika (and maybe now towards me too) from the man she would describe only as "Z". My dad had enough to worry about and I didn't think that his pistol would be much use against a character like that.

What I did was to describe our volunteer work with Maureen, which I thought that he would be proud of. Then I told him about the murder of Maureen's parents, her childbirth, and the interest of the American government in her welfare. This, Randy thought, likely had to do with discovering the identity of the spy who stole America's greatest military secret, which every American spy catcher wanted to find out.

But we weren't spy catchers! We were just two girls, one fourteen and the other nearly fourteen, who were trying to survive a boring summer.

My dad thought for a few moments. Then he told me what I needed to know, which wasn't reassuring. I already knew the limit of what a client could learn from their lawyer no matter how good the lawyer was, and my dad was a very good one. He had said that no lawyer could ever be certain so they always speak in terms of "what should happen" or "what will likely happen." This is because the law is often not clear. There may be many laws governing a crime and a person can be charged under any of them. If a defendant is found guilty, there is a range of sentences which can be imposed.

So my dad always said that the important thing was to never get into court because once there you can't be sure of what will happen. Juries and judges can surprise you so a good lawyer tries to avoid them. What a client wants is a lawyer who knows the law, has good contacts, and is persuasive, and my dad was all three. And though what I asked wasn't his specialty (for he dealt with maritime law which deals with ships), what I learned was helpful but not reassuring.

"Randy is a very smart boy and knows much more about science than I do. He also reads widely and has Internet friends who trust him, so I would take seriously what he said.

"Though it's unlikely that you will discover the identity of this spy, you might. Stranger things have happened, these becoming known decades later if ever. The British breaking of the Enigma coding machine, allowing them to learn German military secrets during World War Two, became public knowledge only forty years after that war ended.

"Now, what could happen if you and Erika are lucky and do get important information from Maureen? And you might, particularly if she trusts you as it seems that she is beginning to.

"First off, you better tell me so I can inform some government people. I've only had one national security legal case and that was before you were born. But I have some old phone numbers and at least one of them will likely still be good.

"To return to your major worry: can you and Erika be charged with a crime for just learning secret information? The answer is no. But prosecutors are politicians too and do bring undeserved charges when they get nervous. The government doesn't like bad publicity. So if what you are doing will cause the government to be seen in a bad light, be careful. You could be charged even if you are entirely innocent and on the side of the angels.

"Not so long ago a celebrated FBI agent was indicted on five felony counts, which could have landed her in jail for a minimum of ten years. Her lawyer plea-bargained this down to a single misdemeanor though she lost her job. What did she do to get into all this trouble? Just what she was ordered: to operate undercover against a family friend who was a suspected Chinese spy. The bureau thought that since she was Chinese she'd more likely be successful.

"I hope that what I'm telling you is scaring you because, to paraphrase what Randy said, you are traveling in deep waters. So let me bore you just a bit more."

I hugged dad. "You never bore me!"

He kissed my forehead again before getting up, walking to a filing cabinet, and returning with a thick yellow folder tied with a red ribbon. He rummaged through it before speaking again.

"There are two statutes which you have to worry about. They're both in Title 18 of the U.S. Code. Section 793 states that if you gain secret information and pass it to someone not allowed to see it, or if you lose it, you could be sentenced to ten years in prison or fined or receive both.

"Section 794 is worse but I can't conceive of how it could apply to you. If you deliver secret information to a foreign government with the intent of harming this country you could be sentenced to life imprisonment or death."

He kissed my forehead reassuringly before ending his lecture, which had turned into a warning. "So I strongly suggest that you share with me any information which you get from Maureen. Both of our families would rather that you and Erika receive medals than spend time in jail."

Chapter 25

Randy was undressing me. First my shirt came off and then my jeans, though he had a problem with that. The zipper in front stuck so he ripped it open and pulled them off me. I'll never be able to wear them again, I thought, as he unhooked my bra. I couldn't stop him because my hands were tied to the bedposts. Then he slipped down my panties and spread my legs. It seemed only a moment until he was on top of me. It hurt and I screamed as he thrust over and over again, trying to penetrate me. Finally, he broke through.

"You think that hurt? Now I'll show you what pain really is," Randy screamed. I had closed my eyes but when I opened them and looked up it wasn't Randy's face I saw but that of a stranger, a grown man wearing a mask. Someone I had never seen before who growled at me, "Thank your father for this." I awoke with a scream.

Thankfully, the door of my room was closed so no one had heard me. My younger sister still had nightmares but I would feel embarrassed to admit to having one. Though, As Erika's psychologist had advised her, a nightmare only indicates that there are scary things you are dealing with, either in your thinking or in real life. This made sense considering how my life seemed to be going, with Maureen and Erika's enemy, "Z."

But why did I have *that* dream? The sex with Randy was probably because it was what part of me wanted which, at fourteen, was certainly understandable. Not that many years ago (OK, in colonial days), girls my age were already mothers. And maybe the reason I fantasized Randy being so rough was because he had been more assertive lately. And my having made myself be tied down in the dream might have meant that I wasn't sure I was ready to have sex.

The masked rapist in the picture could symbolize the danger threatening Erika's family and which she had warned me against and we both now faced.

When I realized all this I calmed down: the message that my nightmare was telling me made sense and understanding this meant that my life did too. It might be filled with idiotic behavior but it did make sense.

Then a thought came to me and I smiled at it: that maybe the reason I use the word "idiot" so often is because I am one!

After that dream I turned on all the lights in my

room and just lay in bed. I would have turned on the TV but since we no longer had a cable connection the only station we could get was the local educational one which, that time of the night, only broadcast information, like what was on the school lunch menu for the following week. Fascinating stuff!

So what I did what was a much better substitute for TV. I read a story from the Sherlock Holmes collection of my father. I tried to find something which that ace detective would consider relevant to Erika's story about what faced us and my dad's warning about jail. This, even though I felt like spending the rest of the night in bed with my head under the covers while clutching a stuffed animal from my baby years.

Sherlock Holmes respected women but didn't seem to like them and forget about him loving them. To me he seemed like the teenage boys we meet: pretending to be superior too girls but really being afraid of them. After all, unlike them we can have babies and some boys will never forgive us for that.

The story I read and thought about, The Red Headed League, concerned bank robbers who set up a phony organization of people with red hair in order to conceal their real goal which was to rob a bank. But Sherlock Holmes wasn't taken in by them and he and

Dr. Watson and the half-competent police Inspector Lestrade manage to capture them.

Volunteering at Rillston Hospital seemed to be changing me. After I began going there I found myself thinking about things more. Before, I didn't often try to figure out why I or other people acted as they did, or to interpret my dreams, as I had just successfully done.

Probably most people don't think about their behavior unless something really big happens. Like they get into an accident or get fired from their job and wonder why. But now I did consider events, and so much that Erika sometimes remarked that I looked spacey, which I guess I did. Even Hillary would say this and she could get really out of it, especially when she was fantasizing about "my Bill."

It might have been the talk with Dr. Bradley which changed me or listening to the ideas which Erika got from her psychologist. I think that it was both of these plus our meetings with Maureen, if you can call them that. I'm not sure what to call them. How would you describe a meeting between two teenagers and a teenage baby?

I seem to be rambling like the typical teenage diary so to get back to the Sherlock Holmes story I was reading. What the bank robbers did was to spin their web, which is what Holmes did, and what I was thinking about the day before when Erika told me about "Z." We needed to spin a web or maybe two. One would be to get Erika and her father off the hook and the other to pull Maureen out from wherever she was at. Two webs, I thought, constructed by the two spiders, Erika and me. One to rescue Maureen, and the other to poison "Z."

Chapter 26

My next day belonged to Hillary. She and Erika mixed like water and oil so I had to visit them separately. Like a mother whose children demanded her total individual attention though Erika was far more grown-up than Hillary.

Her attention that day still focused on Bill, the former president, father of their country and, in Hillary's eyes, the mother of their future son.

"'John' or 'William' would be good names. They sound historic like John Adams or William Penn. A politician needs a simple name that people can remember. It's even better if it has meaning for them."

Hillary saw herself as being a president's mother, living in the White House as had President Franklin Delano Roosevelt's mother. It was a patriotic thought so I didn't argue with her. Why waste my time, I decided, she's three steps from being committed at Rillston Hospital. So I just listened and said, "Yes."

"I'm thinking crazy," she suddenly said, after some moments of silence.

Finally she recognizes it, I thought, but I was wrong.

"Just sitting and talking. I should act on my feelings."

"Huh?" I got that anxious feeling in my stomach which I get before math exams. Dealing with two problems at a time, Erika's and Maureen's, was my limit.

"Yes. I should see Bill and get this show on the road, like they say. It's healthiest to have a baby when you're young. If this was colonial times I'd already have two. A fourteen year old is...." She seemed to struggle for the word, "ripe."

"What...what do you plan to do?" Now I was beginning to stutter like Randy.

"Why see him of course. Introduce myself and let things go as The Lord intended, as it did with Monica."

It didn't seem to me that there was much biblical about what happened between Bill and Monica. My Hillary was reading her own Bible.

I played for time, knowing that it's never good to argue with a lunatic. "Hmm," I murmured.

"Yes. I'll bike to his house in Chappaqua tomorrow. It's only fifteen miles away. I can do it in an hour. Let's decide what I'll wear." Hillary's voice held the certainty of craziness.

I didn't reply. Just let ramble, I said to myself. If

necessary, you can puncture her bike tires before leaving.

She rummaged through a closet and took our several outfits, holding each before me.

"Which would be better? To show him how I really am or what we will have together? Should I dress as the innocent teen or the slutty one?"

I didn't see much difference in either outfit. One, a mini, left nothing to the imagination and would back up traffic. The micro would cause a major accident, probably close down the road for hours.

"No panties," she added.

She'll close down the road for days, I thought.

"Each of them is so...*you*," I said.

"The black one, I think, with a lace top and no bra."

"Take a sweater so you don't catch a chill," I suggested.

"Good idea," she replied with a big smile, being pleased that I was onboard with her plan.

Still, I wondered how serious she was. All teenagers fantasize, like my rape dream of the night before. But having a fantasy and acting it out are two very different things. She'd probably masturbate, have a good night's sleep, and forget about Chappaqua I thought and almost jumped. Masturbate? Having a dream of being raped? What was happening to me?

My conclusion sounded logical and did reassure me but it was totally wrong. Hillary did bike to Bill's (and his Hillary's) home in Chappaqua the next day, and then told me what happened.

"It took me more than an hour. But that was mostly because of a driver who stopped and offered me a lift. He was cute but too old for me."

I wondered how old that would be. Was he ninety-five?

"The town looks a little like Greenwich but it's not as rich. There are no high walls around houses and the people aren't as friendly. I stopped at the local deli which they call The Little Store and had a sandwich which they call a 'wedge.'

"Chappaqua isn't as elegant as Greenwich. I can't see why someone would want to live there, or on Bill's street. There are five houses alongside and it has a short gravel driveway. The house is no bigger than yours though the waitress at the diner said that it has five bedrooms. That's fewer than the house you're inheriting. You won't feel ashamed to have us visit you there."

The last comment was made with a small smile

which might have been a lunatic grin. Dr. Bradley would know.

"I walked on the grounds to look around but was stopped by a guard. I said that I lived nearby and Bill was my idol and that I hoped to get a glimpse of him. The guard said that he worked at his office in Harlem (that's in Manhattan) all week and I was out of luck.

"So I just rode around town and then came back. The whole trip took only three hours. I could visit every day during the summer if I wanted but I had a better idea. His wife or daughter and her husband might be there for the summer so it wouldn't be a good idea to go there again."

I sighed with relief for visiting Hillary in jail wouldn't be fun.

"It would be better to see him at his office in New York. But I can't bike there and will need train fare. Margaret?"

"Not from me. I'm always broke."

We sat facing each other until an idea hit me. Erika and I hadn't yet managed to recruit a babysitter for our business. Hillary could be our first until she got arrested. And flaky though she might be, she was good with kids. My younger sister adored her even if that might not be saying much for the genes in my family.

"You could earn a hundred dollars a day babysitting for us as soon as we get a client. That would more than cover your train fare to New York, which is less than an hour away. The subway fare after that is just two dollars. What do you say?"

Hillary squealed with delight. "I'd do anything for my Bill!"

Poor kid, I thought, and hoped that his guards wouldn't boot her down the stairs before arresting her. I had noticed that Randy enjoyed staring at *her* butt too.

Chapter 27

When I informed Erika that Hillary had signed on as our first babysitter, her reply was brief.

"She's crazy!"

"She's just a little crazy," I agreed. "Every girl gets like that when she's involved with a boy. Look at me and Randy."

"Randy is fourteen. Bill is sixty-four year and married though I will admit that he is still looks great."

"There's a good point to her fantasy. With her head wrapped around Bill, she won't be interested in the father in any home we send her to."

"You didn't mean that as a pun, did you? Like how Monica was with Bill?"

When I realized what Hillary was referring to I blushed. Oral sex was light years beyond what Randy and I would be exploring anytime soon.

"No." I quickly changed the subject. "But we don't have any babysitters and we need one now for our first client: an overnight for a couple who want to relive their honeymoon at the Delamar Greenwich Harbour. They have two young girls."

"That place has child-care available. I stayed there

once with my dad and his then girlfriend."

"Like I said, they want to relive their honeymoon when they didn't have kids."

"Did you meet them? What were they like? I don't want to read a headline, 'Babies Murdered By Bill's Lover.'"

"They're sweet, four and six. All she'll have to do is to read to them or play games , put them to bed, and get breakfast for them and play with them the next morning. The parents will be back by 2PM. What could be easier? She's been doing that with her brothers for years."

"OK, but I think that we should check in on her that evening to be sure everything is OK. And I want to inspect her before she goes. No see-through blouse, and she must wear panties!"

We did inspect Hillary before her babysitting gig and, much to Erika's surprise, she looked OK. Like any fourteen-year-old at a babysitting job and no different from how I dress during the summer: a white shirt, knee length shorts, and white sneakers. The only color in her outfit was her blue scarf and the huge button which was Erika's idea. It read Greenwich Babysitting League, with a phone number under it and a drawing of Snoopy which she had talked her father into licensing for her.

The company was glad to do it as a favor to him. Like my dad, my Aunt Lena, and Erika always say, it pays to know the right people.

Despite Hillary's sensible appearance we did worry, and it took all of our self-control not to check her every hour. We decided to visit her at 7PM, supposedly to bring snacks for everyone. We didn't want Hillary believing that we distrusted her.

On the way over, we (Erika, Abram, and me), driving in the armored SUV with my bike on top, made an important stop: at Greenwich's Black Forest Pastry Shop. My family used to shop there before my father stopped working.

The snacks we bought for the children lay next to Abram in the front seat: three boxes holding a chocolate mousse cake, chocolate truffles, and a half-dozen Smiley Face cookies. Erika paid with her father's credit card and remarked that America was made for doing business.

While sitting in the back row, Erika opened the seating compartment beneath her and fingered one of the machine pistols which was stored there. This gave our babysitting aid mission a surreal appearance.

But no rescue was necessary. Hillary seemed puzzled why we came, and already knew whether the children had any food allergies, which hadn't occurred to us.

This confirmed my opinion of Hillary: that though being temporarily flaky she was a good babysitter.

Since Abram now accompanied us everywhere and the children's parents knew nothing about him, we didn't stay long. Both Erika and I feared that the children might report having seen a strange man, one who might have carried pistol in a shoulder holster though it was well-concealed under his jacket.

But the children were overjoyed with the snacks. I would have liked to take some home but reminded myself that these were a business purchase. Hopefully, with more babysitting clients, my family could again afford to shop at the bakery.

By 7:20PM we were back on the road and I had Erika drop me off at Mother Marie's apartment. Though past eighty and being in good health, I still checked in on her at least once a week though I sometimes wondered who was checking on who since I did most of the talking. I usually had a lot to say, and this visit was no different.

There was no one else who I could tell what most worried me. Hillary was Hillary and I could deal with Randy's anxieties on my own or with advice from my older sister or from Erika. But I had no one to share Erika's problem with, not unless I wanted them to share the danger we faced.

But Mother Marie was an Ifa priestess, an iyanifa, or Mother of Ifa. Surely, with her powers, she could be in no danger.

This is what I hoped as I told her about Erika. The mysterious "Z" who was a business enemy of her father and had taken out his vengeance by ordering the rape and murder of Erika's older sister and mother, and who now threatened her and maybe even me since I knew of his existence.

I would have expected this story to shock Mother Marie but it didn't. She had dealt with many terrors in her long life, which is what a priestess does: relieve pain and extend life just like a doctor.

She knew the two hundred and fifty-six odu, the patterns which can fall when using the divination system known as the diloggún by which the priestess learns the will of the Orisha Gods.

But she didn't perform that ritual this evening. Instead, as was usual, she told me a story, this being how she usually instructed me.

This story was of Oshún, perhaps because his feast day was the following month.

"You know of Oshún's great powers, that she is the owner of all that makes life worthwhile: beauty and love and abundance. But it was not always like this. Once she was poor, like your family.

"She wandered the earth in poverty, feeling so sad that instead of creating wealth she destroyed all that she touched. So she went to a diviner to find out what she needed to do in order to change her life. His message was simple: for her life to change she must give up all of her remaining wealth, an action which would require all of her spiritual faith.

"She was told to use all of her money, down to her last penny, to buy honey and oil which she was to pour into the river.

"Oshún was afraid to do this for she had so little left. But she had faith in God and in the diviner's skill. After pouring the honey and oil into the river she fell into a deep sleep. The wise Orisha, Eshu, then spoke to Olódumare in Heaven: 'see what your daughter has done. She sacrificed all that she had and now cries in her sleep. She was the last of your creations and the health of the world depends on her happiness.

"Olódumare promised to reward her, and when Oshún awoke she found that her tears had turned into tiny diamonds and the riverbank was strewn with jewels. Which is how Oshún became the richest Orisha on Earth. She sacrificed all that she had and God rewarded her faith.

"All that you have, Margaret, is your life, and you are willing to sacrifice this for your friend. You need not fear, for God will protect you."

Then Mother Marie went to a cabinet and brought a yellow and green beaded necklace, the colors of Orula, the God who was present at the beginning of creation and thus knows the past, the present, and the future, along with a set of kola nuts. I understood why. Because of a pact between Orula and Ikú, the personification of death, one cannot die before one's natural time while wearing the necklace.

It was nine o'clock and nearly my bedtime when I left Mother Marie. As I rode my bike home, I felt sure that I would sleep well that night.

Chapter 28

Erika was jumpy when I arrived at her home the next morning for breakfast. Not that my mother liked my missing breakfast with our family, for that and dinner were when we spoke the most as a family. But she and my father accepted that, as their children grew older, they would become more independent. So long as our friends were good ones, meaning that they got good grades and didn't use drugs or sleep around, it was OK with them that we practically lived over their houses. Particularly during the summer which was considered to be our time, days being away from the structure of school, which they also felt was healthy.

Our parents trusted their kids, believing that if a child had been problem-free until becoming a teenager, they were unlikely to do worse then. But I'm not sure that they counted on me.

Like I said in *Margaret of Greenwich,* I am the odd-ball in the family. I look different, being taller than the others, am one of the two with blue eyes and the only one in generations (so my late grandmother had told me) with red hair and the freckles that go along with it.

Margaret and Erika

My Aunt Lena had implied that there was some long ago secret about me which was related to why she and my mother, who was her sister, no longer spoke.

But she refused to tell me what it was although she was my godmother, a role which she had accepted before my mother broke with her.

I'm starting to ramble again so I'll get back to that morning. I noticed that Erika was jumpy when I arrived for breakfast with her. She responded to every slight noise and ate little though I made up for it. We have plenty of food in my home but never the specialties which are in Erika's home on a daily basis.

There are some things I grew to love which we never had: whitefish and grilled salmon and even the most expensive kind of caviar too.

Caviar is simply fish eggs. The type I got used to eating at Erika's home was fresh Beluga which costs about three thousand dollars a pound. The eggs are small and golden in color. Abram told me that this food was once reserved for Russian czars and now, I thought, for Connecticut billionaires.

It's the kind of food one must acquire a taste for and Erika seems never to have developed it. I never saw her father eat it either so he might get it for the bodyguards, who are all Russian. It was Abram who told me how to eat it. You use a small plastic spoon since metal can give caviar a funny taste. Russians take a first taste by putting a bit on the back of their hand, but I never did this. You eat it on crackers or toast.

The first time I ate it, only a little after Abram told me how much it cost, I wondered what other expensive taste this teenager from a poverty stricken family would acquire next!

Erika ate less than usual that morning. Her father had once described her as being "borderline anorectic" though I think he was more annoyed by her lousy eating habits than repeating anything which her psychologist had told him.

I've seen anorectic girls, and one boy too. They are very thin and look scary. They are little more than bones, and wear loose clothes so that others don't see how much weight they have lost. Hillary, who despite being temporarily crazy is my mental health expert, once told me what she knew about anorexia based on her WebMD investigation.

That these people's problem is basically not about food but about growing up. For whatever reason, whether or not to eat had become their way of asserting their independence against their parents, so that anorexia is a family issue too. She also said that it was the mental health condition with the highest death rate and is really something to worry about. This might have been the reason for the concern of Erika's father. Not that she was so thin but that, having lost her mother and sister, he wanted her to grow up healthy.

But Erika just seemed to be one of those people who couldn't eat in the morning though I noticed that she made up for it at lunch and dinner. Her father rarely noticed this since he worked so much and our companions for those meals were usually one or two of the bodyguards.

That morning I noticed more of them about. Most were new, Erika informed me, and were relatives or friends of Abram or Ivan.

"They have a thing about really trusting only family members, which I guess makes sense. Some of them were soldiers who served with Abram, so they're sort of like a family to him. I almost expect them to salute when they meet. They're like that, real military."

The bodyguards were dressed in greenish-blue camouflage and black boots. Several of them had 'VDV' tattoos and I asked Abram about this. Tattoos are strictly forbidden for Mormons, who seem to follow the Jewish and Muslim tradition in this matter. They consider the body to be the temple of God and that it should not be cut or defaced.

"They were in the Vozdushno-Desantnaya-Voyska, the VDV. It's Russia's air assault force, like the American paratroopers," he explained.

But he ignored my next question, which was about the tattoo of a large tiger on several of their left shoulders. It was Erika who later explained this.

"The tattoo means that he killed someone," she said.

Chapter 29

Erika was still jumpy as we drove to Rillston Hospital. Like with most people, eating relaxed me though it had no effect on her. Erika ate because she had to stay well in order to accomplish the two most important things in her life: taking care of her father, and learning as much as she could about his business philosophy and the businesses he owned so that she could one day manage his fortune better than he did. So long as what she ate kept her healthy, food wasn't on her radar and any meal was fine.

Erika kept chattering as we drove to Rillston Hospital. Though what she said was interesting, it wasn't what girls usually talk about. Not clothes or makeup or even boys, but about a deal which her father was putting together though she was careful never to mention names. She always remembered that just the hint of insider trading had gotten people into trouble, and more of that was not what her family needed.

Finally she seemed to wear herself out and became silent, slumping into the comfortable leather car seat. Then she noticed my beaded necklace, the one which Mother Marie had given to me.

"I didn't see that before. It's beautiful. Can I hold it?"

"I can't take it off. It's a religious object. I have to wear it all the time." I thought of explaining that it was intended to keep me safe but saying this would raise questions into her very logical mind about matters which I didn't feel ready to share with her. About Mother Marie and Babaluaiye, my God husband, and the pact between Orula, the God who was present at the creation, and Ikú, who was the personification of death.

So I kept my answers brief and general, to make it seem that wearing the necklace was just another of those silly habits which every teen has. Doing something which made no sense to anyone except its owner and so wasn't worth talking about except maybe with their psychologist. Erika got my message.

"Mormons are complicated people," she remarked, and closed the subject, as I had hoped that she would.

We arrived at Rillston Hospital a little after eleven, and it was a relief to get there. The hospital had always seemed a place of safety to me. This might be because when I was younger and riding my bike nearby, I had fallen and badly scraped my knee. I went in to see Aunt Lena and she had a doctor take care of it. Also, because I always felt that I could rely only on her and my father for unconditional support with problems that arose.

I would talk to my father about an ordinary problem, and with Aunt Lena about those which I was afraid to tell him. Aunt Lena had been expelled from high school for selling marijuana. Now, being respectable and wealthy and a nationally recognized authority on managing hospitals, I felt that she could deal with just about anything.

But even with her I hesitated to share my life with Mother Marie and my God husband, Babaluaiye. Still, I had a feeling that she would understand even this. Aunt Lena had gone from being Mormon to an Evangelical Protestant and finally to Judaism during her several happy marriages. My religious life was just as unusual.

Our arrival at Rillston Hospital brought a surprise. Maureen wasn't sprawled in her room or sitting in a nearby window alcove when we arrived. Instead, she sat in the patient recreation room, playing chess on a laptop. We sat on the sofa beside her, not wanting to intrude and continuing to follow Dr. Bradley's instructions.

"As much as possible, let her do the leading. If she is doing absolutely nothing then you make suggestions.

But people with problems have a sense of what they need to be healed and it's important to allow them this freedom."

So that's what we did. We watched her play chess though it was a game which I had learned years before but could never get interested in. Randy and Erika were great chess players. Why am I putting them together in this thought, I wondered, with my next and troubling one being that I hoped she wouldn't get interested in him.

I quickly pushed this idea from my mind. Erika was the most honorable girl I knew. She would no more make a play for my boyfriend than she would shoplift at the mall.

The chess game was a fast one with every move having to be made within twenty seconds. Maureen was playing someone online and seemed to be winning. A few minutes after we arrived the game was over. I expected that she would begin a new one but she didn't. Instead, there was another surprise. She turned towards us and began speaking. Not in her usual babyish tone but like a real fourteen-year-old and sounding much saner than Hillary.

"You have been good friends to me and I'm grateful. I haven't been much fun."

Erika and I were speechless, being surprised both by the comment and its kindness. And though it wasn't polite, we couldn't help staring. Was this the Maureen we had spoken with just two days before? Either Dr. Bradley was a miracle worker or the Gods had intervened, these seeming the only two possible explanations for the huge change in her behavior.

Erika managed to speak first.

"That's all right. We've both been through some rough times though not as bad as the ones you did."

Now Erika was being kind. What she endured, the rape and murder of her sister and mother and the expectation that these would happen to her, was at least as bad as those which Maureen had experienced. My near murder a few months before paled in comparison, though comparing such horrors is worse than silly.

Maureen studied the room. It was large and looked its age, which was nearly a hundred years. I've seen pictures of mental hospital recreation rooms in movies. Those are bare and filled with metal tables and chairs with a TV blaring.

But the walls of this room were lined with built-in wooden bookshelves filled with the latest novels and classics. Just about anything you might like to read for the hospital even had a staff librarian who filled requests. Patients sat on club chairs or on one of the sofas about the room.

In one corner was a large organ. It gave the room the feel of a church rectory. It was a comfortable room and quiet, for there was no TV, a refuge from the world outside. Here, the dangers were psychological and internal. Very different from outside its walls where Erika had recently fingered a machine pistol, one which, I feared, might soon have to be fired.

Chapter 30

My parents have different personalities. My dad is calm and thoughtful while my mother's anxiety too often gets the better of her. But both agree on one thing about me: that I am more than just a little curious. If I am puzzled about something I won't stop digging until I am satisfied, even if it takes a long time.

Many on the hospital staff were curious about Maureen: few if any other teenager had their parents murdered, their baby missing, and the government involved in their life. So, like them, I and even Erika (who had her own worries) was intensely curious.

So what I did wasn't what Dr. Bradley, her psychologist, does: to hesitantly ask what he wanted to know, or to wait until he was sure that the moment was the absolutely right one before asking. Instead, I just asked. After all, she was a fourteen-year-old just like me and as Erika would be in a few weeks. Teenagers ask each other questions all the time and who knows how to do this better than another teenager.

Maybe if we were sitting in a typical mental hospital, where the staff wore white jackets and the furniture was metal, I wouldn't have. But because my

Aunt Lena owned it, Rillston Hospital had always seemed almost a second home to me. I often biked there for advice and an occasional free meal in the cafeteria where the cooks knew me. I once even brought Hillary with me though I tried to reduce my guilty feeling at doing so by telling myself, more than half seriously, that I was helping to make her comfortable in the hospital where she might soon be a patient.

So, without hesitating, I just asked Maureen the first of several burning questions which I had, thinking that if it made her uncomfortable the worst that would happen would be that she would shut down and not talk. This was also something which Randy tended to do, when I said something which made him nervous.

"Maureen, what's been happening with you?" I began. "You're our age and Erika's cousin too. What happened to your parents, and did you really have a baby?"

You did it, I told myself, when I saw Erika glaring at me. Probably my father would have too, for one of his favorite sayings is that a lawyer never asks a question to which they don't know the answer. But I wasn't a lawyer or a business manager in training: I was just one teenager trying to understand another.

To Erika's and likely what would have been Dr.

Bradley's and my father's surprise, Maureen did respond, after a brief, thoughtful silence and not in a babyish tone.

"I'll tell you over coffee," she said, getting up and walking towards the door. We followed her towards the cafeteria, no longer walking hand-in-hand as we had in days past, not being three kids but three growing-up women.

Mormons don't drink coffee but this was Erika's and it seemed Maureen's favorite drink. I chose my usual orange juice and a whole-wheat bagel. They had just coffee.

When we were seated at a table beside a window, Maureen continued her story. Her speech wasn't continuous. There were starts and stops and tears along the way, which was to be expected considering what she told us. Only a crazy person wouldn't have cried, and we did too, quietly with tears running down our cheeks. Not with the occasional moan which we sometimes heard from a patient in the dining room but with real tears. Like those which Randy shed when he thought that I was dead.

"As you can see, I'm Eurasian," Maureen began. "My father was American, of Swedish descent, and spoke English, while my mother was Chinese and spoke

Chinese. This sounds simple to most Westerners except that it isn't. Chinese is not a language but a family of between seven and thirteen different languages, and a person who can speak one of them often can't understand a person speaking the other.

"It's like living on the border between Texas and Mexico and being unable to understand your neighbor who is a mile away. Most Chinese people speak Mandarin but two hundred million of them speak other dialects: Cantonese, Wu, and Min. The Chinese government wants everyone to speak Mandarin and they are succeeding with children. But languages aren't easy to learn after one grows up and they haven't been successful with older people.

"My mother grew up in Jiangyin City in Jiangsu province where Min is spoken. Some call it 'old Chinese' because of its old pronunciations. Jiangyin is an ancient city, twenty-five hundred years old and a military stronghold because of its important position on the Yangtze River. It's become a wealthy industrial center because of its river location along which goods can be shipped quickly. It is also close to the important economic center of Shanghai. I grew up listening to a favorite pop song of the nineteen thirties by Liu Bannong. He was a famous writer and the words in the song go, 'Tell me how to stop thinking of her.'"

That is a nice tune, I thought, and noticed that Erika had become riveted by Maureen's story. Possibly her father had never heard of Jiangyin and she was reminding herself to inform him of its commercial possibilities.

"I grew up learning Min from my mother and Mandarin from the babysitters she employed. By the time I was seven I was fluent in both languages, and English which was spoken at home. My mother and I spoke only Min when we were alone. My father wasn't good at languages: he always said that New York English was good enough for him, which was a weird thing to say for a guy who lived most of his life outside of the United States."

I became curious again and broke one of my golden rules: to never interrupt a speaker.

"What kind of work did your father do?" I asked.

Maureen was silent for a moment and I began kicking myself. But she soon answered.

"I'm not sure. He had a doctorate in electrical engineering, or maybe it was computer science. I never asked him. It only seemed important later, afterward... "

Now Maureen began crying, sobbing quietly with tears flowing down her cheeks. She wiped them away, caught herself, and continued. She seemed to need to tell her story, not to a psychologist who would analyze her words but to girls her age who would simply be there for her and with her.

"It all began one morning after breakfast. Though my father was as American in his habits as they come, we ate Chinese: typical Jiangsu food which is sweet and not spicy like other Chinese food. We usually had a big breakfast, not much for lunch, and then a large dinner. I can even remember that breakfast for it was our usual: Shengjianbao, which is a pastry filled with beef mince and carrots and cabbage. Because my father didn't like cabbage the cook would make it with onion instead. We also had Matisu, which is fried bread filled with red bean paste and sprinkled with sesame seeds; Dougiang, which is soy milk and, of course, coffee, which none of us could do without though my cup was filled more with milk than coffee. Shengjianbao isn't hard to make. I can teach you."

Maureen rambled on about the ingredients and both Erika and I realized that this was because she was nervous. It was like the rambling that Randy sometimes did. We listened and tried to appear interested though we hungered for the rest of her story.

Chapter 31

"We were having breakfast like on any other day. The doorbell rang. It was a little after eight. No stranger came that early except for the maid and she was already there. She answered the door and then told my father that he had a visitor who said that his matter was urgent. This wasn't a complete surprise since my father sometimes did get visitors that early.

"My father met the man in the study. Then he came back for me since the man spoke just a few words of English. His Mandarin was better but my father's was very poor, also only a few words. The man's native tongue was Min, which I spoke like a native. My mother did too, but she had already left. She was trying to open a modeling agency for young Chinese and had a breakfast meeting at the Verandah room of the Hong Kong Peninsula Hotel. It's our favorite place for breakfast or dinner or whenever. It's a large bright room with ceiling fans and palm fronds and white linen covered tables. My father said that it reminded people of the nineteen twenties."

Maureen began crying and tears again rolled down her cheeks. Abram had been silent as she spoke.

He had been watching her intently though his eyes still glanced about the room occasionally, responding to a noise or something which only he sensed. He once told me that to protect someone you have to look at the people around them and not at them.

We were all, including Abram, moved by Maureen's story and he wiped her tears away with a napkin. Protectively, like a father. Maureen didn't say anything. She just let him do this. When her cheeks were dry she continued her story.

"The man was middle-aged, about fifty. A short man, heavy but not fat. Fit, like a wrestler. He was dressed in a business suit but not an expensive English or Italian one like the men who meet my mother wear. It was a cheap suit but he stood very straight and I had the sense that he would have felt more comfortable in a uniform.

"When my father called me in, the man looked puzzled but my father explained that I was his daughter and could interpret for them, that I had spoken Min since I was a baby and was also fluent in Mandarin.

"Upon learning this the man bowed, took my hand, and said in Min that he was honored to have so beautiful an aide. Then he added an old Chinese proverb: *A drop of water shall be returned with a burst of spring*. This means that you should return even the smallest favor with all that you can when the other is in need.

"I replied with another Chinese proverb: *no one knows a child better than a father*. The man smiled and clapped his hands and bowed again. Then we sat and got down to business.

"This man, he never told us his name, began speaking rapidly and I translated. The story he told was incredible. He worked in a Chinese nuclear weapons program and had access to the storage library which held its secrets. He had gambling debts, his life had been threatened, and his wife needed surgery for breast cancer, for which he had no money. He wanted a new life in America for him and his family, along with five million dollars, guaranteed American protection and citizenship. In exchange he would turn over a duffel bag filled with documents.

"As good faith he showed my father several documents that he had brought. I translated some of the terms on it and my father readily understood the blueprint. One was of a missile warhead and the other was of a new type of electromagnetic aircraft launching system for Navy carriers, using magnets instead of steam. I could see that my father was very excited. I also realized, for the first time, that my father had some type of connection with the American government or the man certainly wouldn't have approached him.

"My father asked him how he had managed to smuggle out the documents and his story was so weird that we were sure it must be true. No one would make up a story like that.

"The man said that he went to the storage area late one night and collected the documents which he put into his duffel bag. His next problem was how to get this large bag past the security guards. What he did was to throw the bag out a second floor window. But the bag broke when it hit the ground and the documents scattered.

"Now the man was really terrified. He was afraid of being caught so he hid in the storage area and smoked a cigarette to calm down. A guard smelled the smoke and asked him what he was doing there. He said that he had been working late and fallen asleep and had a smoke but that he was leaving. He ran down the stairs, collected the papers which had scattered, and put them back into the duffel bag. He got the documents out of China by mailing them to himself using an air courier service.

"The man calmed down after he told us his story.

It was like he had just crossed a raging river and come out safely on the other side. Which in a way is what changing your country allegiance is. My father said he needed approval for the man's request but that he had no doubt it would be granted. He wanted the man to stay with him until then but the man said he had to leave. That he needed to make arrangements for his wife and son to leave China.

"His last words really aroused my father. The man said that many of the secrets he had were stolen from America and that by studying them they might reveal who the spy was. He said that if anything happened to him his friend should be contacted and when his wife and son arrived safely in America his friend would reveal the location of the duffel bag. This man, who he didn't name, worked as a porter at the Four Seasons Hotel.

"Before he left he bowed and stated a Chinese proverb: *Fortune does not come twice.* I replied with another: *people's plans are inferior to the fate of heaven,* meaning that man proposes and God disposes.

"The man smiled, bowed, and we never saw him again."

Chapter 32

We all stared at Maureen, being anxious to hear what happened next. But this had to wait for a moment later a counselor came to the table to remind her of her appointment with her therapist. Maureen left with him, and I thought that Erika and Abram must be sharing the same feeling of let-down which I did. What happened after the Chinese stranger left the apartment? It must have been shortly afterward when the horror in her life began.

We would learn this later, or never. Maybe after her therapy appointment she would be more open, or less. We would have to wait.

But relaxation seemed not to be intended for me. I was called to the receptionist, who had three telephone messages: one was from Randy, the second was from Hillary, and the third was from a Mrs. Holley, who I didn't know.

Hillary and Mrs. Holley must be about business, I decided, so I called Randy first. He needed me, was my boyfriend and, though he didn't know this yet, was my future husband and the father of our children. Like people say: family comes first.

"Where are you," Randy screamed into the phone.

"I'm obviously at Rillston Hospital, and with Erika. I told you that we were volunteers here."

"I need you."

It was good that he recognized this, I thought, and maybe that I should pause before answering him. But I'm not that kind of girl. I don't play games, which may be a mistake. So I simply said that I needed him too.

Then I asked, "What's wrong? You sound upset." This was an understatement.

"It's my mother's bright idea. She's having a Caesarean and wants me and my father present when the baby comes. To bond us all, she says. I can't!"

No, Randy couldn't, though his father would never accept this. Randy's father was a big-time surgeon who loved to operate. Getting his hands bloody was the equivalent of my getting smudged fingers from a printer. It didn't bother me.

But Randy could never be a doctor, which was the career his father intended for him. He was ambitious but his head was into science and computers and I expected that someday others beside me would know how great he is. This had already begun.

Months before the FBI, upon learning what we had been up to, hustled a college scholarship before his eyes. Which, being a steady government job, might be a good career option. But medicine was not a possible career for Randy. He couldn't stand the sight of blood and certainly not to get it on his hands though I knew that he must know that menstruation involved bleeding for he was into sciences.

Randy even had to drop out of biology lab though he was the smartest student there. He couldn't touch the animal which we had to dissect. So his mother went behind her husband's back and got a doctor's note excusing him from the lab, stating that he was allergic to the preservative chemical or something. Knowing this, why she would want him to witness her childbirth was beyond me. Or maybe it was his father's idea, to try to get the fear out of him. Which I guess is how surgeons are: aggressive and wanting to do something immediately to solve a medical problem. Waiting for change isn't their style.

But if Randy was so afraid of blood, how would he deal with my monthly period? I'd have to be sure to hide the bloody tampon and be sure that not a drop of blood was on the toilet seat. The sight of either would freak him out. And forget about him ever diapering our children. He might not even be able to tolerate the sight of me breast feeding. Randy, I said to myself, the things that we girls have to put up with to get a family.

"Don't worry, Randy, that's months away. We'll do something. I promise you."

"OK, OK," he said, and I could hear that he was gaining control of himself. "When am I going to see you?"

"I'll see you tonight. Come over for dinner. Then we'll watch a movie." That was the code phrase I used for us doing you know what.

"Love ya," he said, and hung up, before I had a chance to reply. Boys!

Mrs. Holley turned out to be a new customer for our babysitting business. She was a single, newly divorced parent of a five year old boy and an eight year old girl. The parents shared custody and lived close by. Both would be away on business trips the following weekend and they needed a babysitter. I agreed to meet her that afternoon for an interview.

I returned Hillary's call last. She just wanted to chat.

"I don't think it would be good to surprise Bill by showing up at his office," she gushed, in the husky tone she was now trying on.

I listened sympathetically. She was our only babysitter and our business needed her here, not in jail.

"No," I said, in an equally soft tone. I'd try my husky tone with Randy later. "What are you thinking of?" I asked, beginning to feel anxious. Or maybe it was my being in a mental hospital which was making me jumpy.

"I'll introduce myself by sending him candy and flowers. I'll sign the card, 'From Your Hillary.' Then when we actually meet it'll be like we've known each other for ages."

He'll probably fall down, I thought, or get another heart attack. I wondered how many Hillary's he had in his life. Then again, with Hillary, his present wife, being Secretary of State and traveling around the world, it might be months before he found out that it wasn't she who was sending him the presents. Before then, he might not mention it over the phone. For all I knew, it might even improve their marriage.

Though Hillary's current idea was a safer one than just showing up at his house, I didn't want to openly agree. Doing this could make be an accessory before the fact, as my dad might say. I'd have to check this with him first. So I just murmured, "Hmmm," and let her interpret this as she would. It wouldn't sound so bad if the feds were bugging her phone after hearing of her trip to Chappaqua. Maybe to them a love threat was the same as a death threat. Another question to worry my lawyer-father.

Now Hillary brought up the real reason for her call. "I need money for the presents. Do you have any more babysitting jobs?"

The Gods must be favoring me, I said to myself, as I thought of our newly arrived client.

"We may have a great new job. One lasting all weekend which means at least forty-eight hours pay. You'll watch two delightful children: a five-year-old boy and an eight-year-old girl. You'll love them. I'm meeting the mother later today."

"A boy," Hillary gushed again, "like my son with Bill."

My lunatic, I thought. What if Hillary decided that this child was hers? This I would have to check out with Erika. It was better to lose a client than to endanger a child.

I went looking for Erika in the cafeteria. We had a lot to talk about, and I couldn't wait to hear the end of Maureen's story.

Chapter 33

They were where I had left them. Erika cradled the coffee cup in her hands, as if it were winter instead of summer and she was trying to get them warm. Abram didn't eat when he was on the job. He was scanning the room and occasionally looking thoughtfully at Erika. As if she were his child rather than his employer's daughter and another boss. Which, though not yet fourteen, Erika certainly acted, and as if she were my boss too.

But I didn't object since she knew lots more about setting up and managing a business than I did. Though her family wasn't religious and she never attended church so I did have God on my side. But as my mother was prone to say, you don't rely on God to handle what you can do. Or as Erika would decide, which is why I planned to run our new problem by her.

"I'm not sure about Hillary babysitting a boy," I began. "She's got this thing about giving birth to Bill Clinton's son. What if she decides that the boy who she's babysitting is theirs and runs off with him?"

"Then you and I will become the most famous business managers in the world and the Greenwich Babysitting Registry will crash and burn. We'd probably be sued too which is why I insisted on making our business a corporation. All they could get is what the company has in the bank which is maybe fifty dollars.

"Some workers can be pretty crazy off the job but still be good while there. One of my dad's accountants is a real Looney Tune but a great accountant. He manages to split off his craziness from the rest of his life. Hillary is probably the same. You said she was good with kids. When she's with them she probably becomes like a kid but also keeps enough sense to take care of them.

"If it would make you happier we can check her out and this would be good public relations. We'll tell the mother that we evaluate our babysitters while they're on the job to be sure that they're living up to our high standards. I'm sure no other babysitting business does this."

Was I right when I said that Erika was a business genius? If, years from now, you hear of a company she's running, run and buy stock in it. You won't regret it for if she thinks like this at thirteen, can you imagine how she'll be in ten years!

That became our plan and was what I told Mrs. Holley, though her reaction scotched my plan to evaluate Randy's suitability for being a parent.

"Impressive, but I don't want a boy coming over.

This is not your babysitter's play date."

"Never," I assured her, though I felt that Randy would be more than a little disappointed. He had never played doctor with me when we were young but was now more than willing to play house.

Maureen arrived a few minutes later. She looked about like she had when she left us and maybe even a little happy. She never talked about her therapy but it had obviously done her some good. She got a coffee at the counter before joining us, which was another good sign. She was behaving more like a living creature than the droopy rag doll she had been.

Abram stood as a sign of respect when she arrived, and she smiled. She actually smiled, though it was a brief one.

No one spoke though we all hungered to know what happened after the Chinese man left the apartment. Maureen sipped her coffee until the cup was three-quarters full, and then continued her story.

"My dad called someone after the man left. Then we continued our breakfast as if nothing unusual had happened. That wasn't the first time I was his interpreter but with the other people it involved simple courtesies, nothing about secrets and weapons.

"The doorbell rang, the maid answered, and three

men burst in. They wore business suits but their faces were concealed by ski masks. They ordered us to sit and eat as if nothing had happened and we did. Their pistols convinced us.

"The maid was nearly hysterical so they took her into the other room and I heard her fall to the floor. But my father and I continued eating as if it were just another morning. It's strange how the mind works. Part of it told me that I might die at any moment but another part of me was waiting to be rescued though by whom I had no idea. The Marines are already on their way, I told myself, like in the American movies of the Old West.

"The men were apparently waiting for someone or something but I tried to ignore them and continued eating. A bite of Shengjianbao, the beef pastry, then a sip of Dougiang, the soy milk. I took one bite after another in a rhythm. I thought of throwing the hot coffee into the face of one of the men and grabbing for his gun but quickly realized that because there were three of them this wouldn't work. My father's eyes seemed to warn me against this too.

"We continued sitting and eating. Chewing and sipping, while the men stared at us. Though I couldn't make out their facial expression because of their masks, I had the impression that they weren't angry with us or even felt anything. They were just doing their job, which to them was an ordinary one. Like being a suit wearing bank official but these men were obviously stronger than the typical office worker.

"An hour later I heard the outer door open and it quickly became clear what the men had been waiting for: the arrival of my mother.

"As we left the apartment I saw the body of the maid on the floor. It was covered with blood. They hadn't knocked her out but had killed her quietly with a pistol with a silencer. Our long journey was about to begin."

Chapter 34

"There was no way to resist for the men held pistols in their coat pockets. We were shuffled out of the building into the back of a waiting white panel truck. Once there, we were blindfolded, our mouths were taped, and our hands were tied with plastic strips behind our backs. I was terrified. My parents' lives and mine seemed over. The maid's life had been ended in an instant and ours could be too.

"I had no idea who they were or what they wanted, whether one of them was the boss or they were simply hired thugs who knew as little as we did. Criminals who had been ordered to pick us up and deliver us, which is what they were doing efficiently.

"The three of us sat in one row and they sat on the opposite side. No one spoke."

While Maureen spoke, people entered and left the cafeteria but, apart from Abram's continued watchfulness, we didn't notice. Nor did we pay attention to the drinks on the table though Maureen sipped hers from time to time.

"Part of me was thinking clearly and part was looking at things like a child," Maureen continued. "The child part wanted to yell for my parents to do something. The grown-up part knew that they were helpless, accepted this situation, and trying to think of some way out. I tried to think of something I could do to help but nothing came to my mind. We were like cattle being taken to the slaughter yard.

"Several Chinese proverbs came to me and they seemed to sum up our situation and my hopes too. *A gem is not polished without rubbing, nor a man perfected without trials. A child's life is like a piece of paper on which every trial leaves a mark.*

"We waited. After not very long the van stopped, our blindfolds were removed and the plastic bands were cut, and we were taken from the van. We were at what looked like a private airport. Several hundred yards away stood a waiting jet, a Learjet. I recognized it because I had flown on one. A friend of my father's took us to Shanghai for the weekend. This jet had the same oatmeal colored seats as the other.

"Things were more relaxed once we got on the plane. We sat on a sofa while the three kidnappers sat facing us. When I had to pee one of the men took me to the lavatory but left me alone inside it. I looked around for any kind of weapon, even a discarded plastic kitchen knife, but there was none. There was no way out.

"We were fed chicken sandwiches and cold tea, not hot tea which we might throw in their faces. Even cattle are fed on the way to their slaughter.

"But I sensed that we weren't to be killed. This could have been done easily in our apartment. No, we were being taken somewhere for questioning, which likely involved being tortured too.

"I had seen movies of torture during a weekend sleepover at a friend's home. She was into this stuff which I called 'torture porn' and couldn't stomach though the other girls loved it but they were older. One was Nakagawa's *Jigoku* of fifty years ago. It had many scenes in which there was the cutting off of body parts as it described the Buddhist underworld.

"There were also the recent movies from the *Scream* and *Saw* series. All disgusted me and I went home early. I told my mom who wondered about their parents but I said that parents don't always know everything that their kids are doing. This caused her to give me a look though we both knew that what I said was true and not that I was into anything bad.

"While chewing my chicken sandwich and looking at my father, I began wondering about the kind of work he really did. I knew that it involved computers and math for he was great at helping me with my homework though I didn't have the problem with math that most girls seem to have for math was my best subject. But did he really work for the insurance company as he said he did? Could he be working for the American government? Was he a spy? Did my mother know (how could she not?), and was she a spy too? Was the modeling agency she was starting up real, or a cover for spying activities? It could be a great one with its world-wide traveling opportunities and the need to meet many people in the ordinary course of business.

"These crazy possibilities had never before entered my mind but now seemed true. Why else would the Chinese man have sought my father? A person wouldn't approach just anyone with his strange request.

"This thought made me feel better. If my dad worked for the government then we weren't alone. They could—would—send someone to rescue us.

"It was that hope which helped to keep me calm, along with the matter-of-fact way in which my parents were relating to that morning's craziness. My mother held her arm about me and my father looked reassuringly at me. The kidnappers wouldn't let us talk. When my father tried, one of them simply pointed a pistol at him and we both got the message.

"We were in the air for a little under four hours

before the plane started to land. I looked out the window and could see a large city but knew that I had never been there. I would have remembered. There was a tall red tower and a large bridge."

Now Abram spoke for the first time. "You were in Tokyo. That was the Tokyo Tower and the Rainbow Bridge. The Tower is taller than the Eiffel Tower and the Bridge is lit up at night. Both are world famous."

"Yes, I learned that later. When we met the boss he told me."

Since Abram had made a comment without upsetting Maureen, I thought that it would be OK for me to do so too.

"Was he Japanese?" I asked.

Maureen nodded her head. "No, he was blond like Abram and they had the same accent.

"A Russian," Abram said softly, almost to himself.

Chapter 35

"The plane landed at a small airfield. When we got off we were forced into a small panel truck with Japanese characters on its sides. After a twenty minute drive the truck slowed and went into what seemed a gravel driveway. When it stopped we were led to a small house which was down the road from a much larger house. There was a large center room. In it were a table and chair with restraining straps and several metal tables covered with tarpaulins. On the sides of this room were four smaller rooms. Each had a sturdy door and peephole, like you see in prison movies.

"We were placed separately into these rooms. There was a toilet, a small sink, a built-in concrete bed with a cheap mattress, and a chair in the corner which was bolted to the floor. There was no window but there were heating or air-conditioning vents high up along two of the walls. The room was chilly.

"Nothing happened for an hour. Then the blond man entered the room. He said that he did not wish to harm either me or my parents but required information they had. He said that as soon as they provided this, we would be flown back to Hong Kong, that tomorrow we might have breakfast in our own apartment as if nothing had happened. It all depended on my parents.

"I listened and said nothing. I thought it would be best to appear as if I were just a dumb, twelve year old. Who pays attention to what they say or think?"

"He brought me American magazines and a Nintendo to make me happy, as if anything could. I guessed that he was trying to make me his ally in the battle with my parents."

Erika hurriedly interrupted her. "You were twelve when this began? So you were a prisoner for nearly two years?"

"Yes," Maureen replied softly, almost with shame.

"My cousin, how you've suffered," Erika said with anguish, gripping Maureen's hand and holding it throughout the remainder of her story. I wanted to comfort her too, being unable to imagine how I could have survived her experience. I took her other hand.

Abram's face tightened. I would not have wanted to be the object of his rage.

"Nothing happened on the first day. That night I was given T-shirts and jeans and a tray of American food. A ham and Swiss cheese sandwich, a banana, and milk. I was fed regularly, morning, mid-day, and in the evening. That was how I managed to keep track of the days. I made a tiny tear on a magazine page for each day that passed. Otherwise I would have no way of knowing how long I had been a prisoner.

"It was on the second day that they began torturing my parents. At first I could only hear their screams. Then I guess they thought it would be more effective to have me witness it, and to imply that I would be tortured next. So they tied me to a chair and gagged me and forced me to watch until I fainted. It got to a point where I could almost force myself to faint.

"My parents' screams grew louder and eventually they did talk but it wasn't what the blond man wanted to learn: the location of the stolen plans. So he had them keep increasing the voltage of the shock box...until they died. My mother died first though she knew nothing. She had been out the morning that the Chinese man came to our apartment.

"When I awoke from the last time I fainted, after both my parents were dead, I found myself not in my cell but in a well-furnished bedroom. The blond man raped me that night. I guess he liked young girls. I was his concubine, he said. It went on like that every night.

"When my periods started a maid told me what to do. Four months later I found myself pregnant. When I started showing, he came less often. We still had sex but not the usual way though he seemed pleased that I was pregnant. 'His wife can't have children,' the maid told me. 'You pleased him.'

"A doctor came to deliver the baby and I nursed him for five months. Then one morning I was told to dress and that I would be sent home, as if I still had a home.

"I was blindfolded and taken to a car. They threw me out in front of the American embassy in Tokyo. I told the Marine guard that I was an American and that my parents had been tortured and killed. He looked at me like I was crazy and I thought that he wouldn't let me in. Being Eurasian I was not like the typical American they see. But I was obviously a child so he asked for my name and called inside and then things happened very fast.

"My father had been an overseas employee of a government agency and they thought that we were all dead. The victims of a random burglary went wrong though Hong Kong is a very safe city. I was so relieved to be with Americans again that I started crying and babbling in Chinese which no one understood. I was hysterical.

"They got a doctor who gave me an injection and I stayed at the embassy until they flew me here. But I didn't want to leave. My beautiful blond son was still there and my breasts were filled with the milk he needed."

At this point Maureen's calm broke down and she began sobbing quietly, not loudly as occasionally happened with hospital patients in the cafeteria.

Then Erika got the look on her face that I had noticed before. As if she were thinking about and weighing things, not dreamily but with intelligence and purpose. Finally she decided.

Her grip tightened on Maureen's hand as she said, "My father will do whatever it takes to bring your baby home. When you leave the hospital you will live with us. You are part of our family."

There are moments in life when one feels that a great and fine thing is at hand. Like a general on the morning when they sense that victory is coming. That was what I felt as the four of us sat in the cafeteria. I felt sure that Maureen's son would be rescued, and that I would play an important role.

Though we hadn't been running around, I was worn out and wanted to leave. I hungered for my home or Erika's, and to speak of ordinary teenage things, if we still could. But Maureen had another surprise for us.

When she stopped sobbing, after Abram dried her

tears, she looked as us pleadingly, as if seeking forgiveness.

"It was only after my therapy session this morning that I suddenly remembered. The Chinese man *did* tell me the name of his friend who is holding the duffel bag with the secret files but in the excitement that morning I translated wrong and didn't tell my father.

"The name is still in my memory but I can't remember it. I feel so guilty. If I had told the kidnappers that name it would have saved my parents' lives.

"What is even worse is that I feel I love their murderer–the man who raped me!"

Chapter 36

I looked at Erika. Both she and I wanted to reassure Maureen but didn't know what to say. Randy's worries about his parents or mine about my dad's health were in a different league. It was Abram, who usually said little, that rescued us. Telling Maureen more than probably even her therapist did. She may not have told him what she had told us, friends and therapists being in different leagues.

"What you feel is not unusual," Abram began. "If you had told him the name then you would have been killed too and not only your parents. It's safer not to leave witnesses and they couldn't have released you after what they had done.

"You did what you had to do to survive, and your feeling of love for this monster is also normal. He controlled what you needed to live and by not taking your life he also controlled it.

"You were kept isolated and knew nothing of the outside world. The horror that you saw—your parents being tortured and murdered—blasted your memory and whatever roots you felt. Then there was the rape, with your body being invaded and violated.

"This man may, at times, have behaved kindly towards you so you could submerge your rage towards him, trying to keep on his 'good side' to protect yourself. And giving birth to his child created another conflict for how could you hate the father of the child you loved?

"You must forgive yourself and concentrate on getting your child back. Do you remember anything about this man beside his hair being blond? Think back! You saw him almost every day for two years. Was there a mark on his body?"

Maureen again became calm after Abram spoke. Her past was gone: regaining her son was what was important.

"He had two tattoos: a spider web on his left elbow, and a rose on his chest," she said softly.

Abram looked at her with wonder. "You're very lucky to have survived. The spider web means that he is a highly ranked killer, and the rose means that he is a member of the Russian Mafia."

Chapter 37

Now I was battling the Russia Mafia, I thought, and wondered how my life could get worse. Maybe Erika was thinking this too because she didn't speak. None of us did. We just listened to the babbling voices in the room, and occasionally touched our cups but didn't raise them to our lips. My mouth suddenly became dry though not from thirst. It was the anxiety which I always felt before a math exam. But this time I got pains in my stomach too. My period had been two weeks before so I didn't think it was that. No, I told myself, the pain is from fear, just normal fear. Only a crazy person would not be afraid when facing what we did.

But then another thought came into my mind, that of a spider's web. I first thought of this when Erika had told me of her father's enemy, "Z." Now I thought of it again and wondered if this was a simple coincidence: my lawyer-father had always distrusted them and he was usually right. Then I had a new thought: that perhaps the Gods, who are strictly moral, hate injustice and punish severely, had now become involved.

Mother Marie had told me stories of Orisha priests who suffered greatly after conducting rituals for evil people. In one case, all of the man's wealth was taken away. But they left him his shop from which he earned a living. The Gods did not want to punish the man's children by depriving them of what they needed.

So perhaps the goals of Maureen and Erika and her family, to regain Maureen's child and to end the threat from "Z," weren't as hopeless as I had feared. Surely no human could defeat the will of the Gods? Elegguá, the guardian of fate and the unexpected; Aganyú, who controls enemies; and, of course, Oyá, who protects against death and controls the burial grounds.

I touched the beaded necklace which Mother Marie had given me and prayed that this was true.

We didn't sit for long. Maureen had a group therapy session though she didn't consider this helpful. The other group members were grown-ups and their problems, except for an ex-soldier's, were very different from hers. He was only nineteen but had already fought in Afghanistan. There, he had experienced many shootings and bombings and seen too many body parts. He had many friends who were killed, and been prescribed too many psychiatric drugs. His doctor at Rillston Hospital took him off them soon after he was admitted.

Now he slept better even with his nightmares,

which had been explained to him.

"They're just me trying to help myself become normal again. People make up their dreams to tell themselves about their life. But with pictures which you have to figure out like you do the plot of a mystery movie. They no longer scare me."

But even with this information Maureen's nightmares still frightened her though she didn't tell them to the group. She knew that what she told to her therapist, Dr. Bradley, would remain with him, and that neither Erika or I or Abram would ever reveal what she had told us. But she couldn't trust the members of her therapy group though she liked them. Who could be sure what they would gossip after they left the hospital. And if what they said found its way back to Maureen's kidnappers, what might be their reaction: to murder her or her son?

So Maureen just listened during her therapy group. This was fine with the group leader and group members, who always had a lot to say. They also enjoyed having a decorative member like Maureen, as the soldier once described her.

"He wants to date me," Maureen told us. "But I'm too old for him."

We understood. The soldier would soon be ready

to return home and to be a teenager again. But, though just fourteen, Maureen was a mother and thought like a grown-up. She had never been a teenager and never would.

It was time for us to go. "Is there anything you need? Can I bring you anything?" Erika asked her.

"My son," Maureen replied simply. That was all she needed. No one could return her parents but her son still lived.

"*We will, we will,*" Erika replied, in an equally soft voice and, without thinking, I touched my necklace again.

We left the hospital just after three. Maureen looked tired and I felt worn out but Erika seemed to have regained her energy. Any new project gave her a jolt though it just added to the several others with which she was already involved.

"Let's talk to Mrs. Holley and check out her kids. Then you can check out Hillary. Do a 'mental status exam,' like the shrinks say. And we have to get more babysitters: relying on her won't cut it. Even if she can stay sane for a weekend, she might get sick. Physical, that is."

Erika didn't like Hillary and we both knew that it would be better for me to speak with her alone. It made no sense to me that Erika could be so kind and warm and understanding with Maureen and the others she did volunteer work with yet be so hostile towards Hillary. Maybe, I thought, because their suffering was obvious and Hillary's was hidden within her crazy thoughts about Bill Clinton, though both were no less real.

Though we never said this openly, we both accepted that I was the one to deal with Hillary. I could tell her whatever I wanted so long as I left Erika out of it.

As Abram courteously opened the door of the SUV for us, his two heavily accented words made a good summary of our afternoon: "Big business," he said.

Chapter 38

Mrs. Holley's house was three miles from the center of Greenwich. The grass needed mowing and the flowers looked wilted. Erika noticed this too.

"I guess that her husband doesn't come around too often, or maybe he no longer cares," she observed.

I didn't say anything. One could make the same criticism of my house though the fault wasn't my dad's but mine. Caring for the lawn was my chore and one which I did badly. I'll never make a good housekeeper, I thought. Randy would either get used to this or he'd do more than half of what needed to get done after we were married.

Erika suggested that Abram wait in the car, saying that the presence of a man might scare a single woman. Another reason for this was that, though appreciating his attention she was, as she put it, tired of having his face up her ass. Abram was also much too good looking to parade before a newly divorced woman.

I suggested to Erika that Abram wear a wedding ring but there seemed no tactful way to tell him this. Russian men, she told me, had a thing about their masculinity, and a boss could only intrude so far into their employee's personal life.

Abram objected to waiting in the car but went along with it. He gave Erika a small personal alarm to press in case of trouble and she promised to hold it in her hand with her finger beside the button. I fantasized she accidentally pressing it and Abram breaking in the door with a machine pistol cradled in his arm. That would end our babysitting business for sure.

Erika rang the bell and Mrs. Holley quickly opened the door. Erika introduced us and began our sales talk, or spiel as she colorfully put it. Though looking innocent, Erika knew many crude and obscene ways to describe business practices. She probably learned these from her father, I thought, though he never used them when I was present.

"We like to meet the children first, to get the best fit with our babysitters. Not every babysitter is good with every child," Erika said.

If I were a mother Erika's statement would have impressed me. But since Hillary was our only babysitter with me being the backup in a pinch, it was far from true. Still, who was I to question the business practices of a billionaire's daughter.

Mrs. Holley's children were, to put it tactfully, monsters. When we arrived the five-year-old kept running from his eight-year-old sister who swore that she would pull his hair out for cutting up her scrapbook. The boy claimed that she had done it but was blaming him to get him into trouble.

I already had the headache which Mrs. Holley probably got frequently. Though in her early thirties, she already had wrinkles in her forehead.

"We have *just* the babysitter for your children. Hillary has a world of patience and all the mothers love her. I'll schedule her for you this weekend and my assistant, Margaret, will be checking in regularly to see if she needs help."

Mrs. Holley smiled at Erika's firm business-like tone. It also so scared the children that they quieted down immediately. I noted my demotion from business partner to assistant but didn't say anything.

Apparently Erika felt that it would be good to leave as quickly as possible and while the children were still calm. I got the impression that Erika didn't like kids for they interfered with her need for order. Another fantasy of mine was that were she their babysitter she might order Abram to shoot them. Well, that's why she's the boss and not a worker, I reminded myself.

"I'll talk to Hillary," I promised Erika as we left the house.

She just nodded, apparently having been a bit shattered by the children's behavior which seemed pretty normal to me. "Two monsters," she muttered as we entered the SUV.

I figured it would be better to tell Hillary about this babysitting job sooner than later, just in case I sensed that she couldn't handle it and I would have to take her place.

She was lying on her bed in the same place as when I last saw her two days before. Still mooning about her Bill, I was sure. Her eyes were closed and I didn't think that what she was fantasizing could be shared with the children I just left.

I sat down heavily on the bed to jar her awake. She opened her eyes.

"Why hello Margaret," she said dreamily, quickly moving her hand from her crotch to her side.

I got down to business. "I saw the two kids you'll be babysitting this weekend. They're pretty active." I quickly described the scene.

"No problem. We'll get started making ice cream sodas and then we'll play games. I'll do the girl's hair while he watches the first *Star War* movie which I'll bring. It came out thirty years ago but I think it's the best episode and kids love it too. We'll have fun."

I was pleased by my earlier conclusion that, although being flaky, Hillary was a good babysitter. This was something which Erika had missed. I'd talk to her about my promotion back to co-manager.

"Stay and have supper with us," Hillary suggested. "I'm now a vegetarian like you."

"I can't, my mom expects me. How come? You practically live at McDonalds."

"No more. Bill's become a vegan. That's a super-vegetarian. He loved fast-food too but after his heart surgery... You have to give your man what he needs! Did you know that vegetarian men have healthier sperm?"

"I must have missed that lesson in science," I replied, but Hillary missed my sarcasm.

I looked back toward her as I closed the door. Her dreamy look had returned. "Bill" was undressing her again.

Chapter 39

My next day's attention belonged to Hillary but she didn't need me as much since she got her Bill. Their relationship existed only in her mind but that was enough for now. Some marriages last because the husband and wife work in separate cities and meet just on weekends. While the "marriage" between Hillary and her Bill might last a lifetime, I hoped that it wouldn't.

Hillary was luscious and Bill might still be impulsive but no one ever accused him of being dumb. Beneath her flakiness, Hillary was smart and, judging by her suggestions the day before, would make a good mother though I doubted that her children would bear the name of Clinton.

On that day I felt free of responsibility to Hillary or Erika or Maureen, and decided to focus on myself. I stopped worrying about "Z" and atomic secrets and the Russian Mafia. I was a kid from a poor family who was about to start eighth grade in the best school in the richest town in America. That was all I wanted: just to be a kid.

So when I got up I stayed in bed until my mother asked if I was well. My usual summer routine had been to be out of the house and on my bike by eight-thirty.

"I'm fine, mom, just taking it easy." Then I noticed that my mother didn't look fine. "How are you?" I asked, though I didn't expect an honest answer. Not that she lied, but parents try to keep family troubles from their children. They feel that it is their job to do the worrying and to let their children grow up with the happy childhood everybody reads about but few actually have. But that day my mom was honest. She started crying.

"I'm not well. I won't be getting the part-time secretary job in the high school which I had last school year. They had budget cuts and people were let go so things will be harder for us this year. I hate for you girls to go without. I haven't told you as often as I should have but I would never change my children for any other."

It was hard for me not to cry too though tears did start to well in my eyes. But I don't like to cry in front of other people. Maybe someday I'll figure out why.

I hugged her so she couldn't see my tears and said, "You are the best mother. We have the best parents and even with our problems I wouldn't live anywhere else."

But even as I said this I realized that it wasn't completely true. Having Erika as a friend had changed me. Wouldn't I prefer to live her life style with golden caviar and imported smoked salmon whenever I wanted and to have a chauffeur driven SUV at the ready? Of course, but not if I also had to deal with her other issues: having just a father with his parade of girlfriends; and the death threat and continuous fear of being kidnapped. It was better to be poor than having those things to cope with.

But I couldn't tell my mother these thoughts. If she knew, she would never let me see Erika. However I did have news which would cheer her up.

"Erika and I have started a babysitting business and we already have several clients. It's only for the Greenwich area and we check out the families we deal with so it's safe. We won't be doing the actual babysitting but will be hiring teenagers to do it.

"With any luck I'll be able to help out a bit. The business may even turn out big if we can find enough babysitters but that's a problem. Most teenagers here have too much money so that now our only employee is Hillary."

My mother's eyes brightened though more from pride in my accomplishment than because of the money. This is what she said before turning the conversation to my future.

"If your father still had his law practice we could send you and your sisters to almost any college. Though maybe not to an Ivy League school unless it gave some scholarship money. Paying sixty thousand dollars a year is more than a bit much for most families, and I'm not sure that the schools are worth it."

"I don't think so either," I agreed, and told her about research I had read on the Internet which showed that the college you graduated from had little to do with your career success. Being bright and motivated and a hard worker was more important.

"There are many good Mormon colleges where the cost is low and you could get a good education and be with your kind of people."

I smiled and said nothing. That my mom suggested this indicated she didn't know me very well at all. But she was trying and I loved her for it. I would have felt closer to her and be more open about my life if she shared more about hers. But, as I had realized years earlier, she couldn't. Not with me and, I suspected, not even with my father.

Randy and I would have a different marriage, I vowed or, as Aunt Lena said she did with her unsatisfactory boyfriends, I'd give him the boot and keep looking.

Someone could appreciate me for who I was and maybe even forgive me for the trouble I tended to find. He must be out there...somewhere.

My mom looked better as she left the room though I felt vaguely dissatisfied. Yes, I loved her. Yes, she did her best as a mother. But also yes, I sometimes wondered how it would be to have Aunt Lena as my mother instead.

I lay in bed and didn't want to get up. Maybe I would watch movies from my sister's DVD collection of old classics, or even read a book. Except for the Sherlock Holmes story I hadn't done that since school ended.

It was nice lying in bed without any responsibilities, I thought, just as one of them rang.

"I'm coming over," Randy said. Any other time I would have welcomed him but that day I couldn't take dealing with another person's problems. There must be times in a dating relationship when it's the boy who should be supportive but no boy seems to know that. Ever super smart ones like Randy.

"Please Randy, not today," I replied, and my statement seemed to throw him. I had never turned him down before, except when he was pushing for having sex which, I felt if we had, we'd both regret an hour later.

"What's wrong? Are you sick?"

"Not sick, I'm just worn out. I'll be OK later. I just want to sleep."

"I'm tired too. We can sleep together."

"You don't sound tired and we can't sleep together. Not now, or in my house," I replied, feeling annoyed at being pressured but also pleased that he made the suggestion. I gave up. "What's wrong?"

"Does something have to be wrong for me to want to see you?" he asked angrily.

Do I have to say it? Boys can be crazy. Sometimes nothing which a girl does is OK with them. The thought of being a single career woman and buying a sperm donor went through my mind, but only briefly. I gave up.

"Come over." I said.

I washed, dressed in my usual, had my usual breakfast (oatmeal, milk, toast, an orange), and waited downstairs.

Randy didn't waste time. He tossed a book on the sofa beside me. "You look. I'll die. I can't do it."

The book was a photo album of Cesarean birth or, as it is popularly called, C-section. Being a star biology student I found the text and photos fascinating but they made Randy seriously nauseous. He had held the book as if it were poison ivy and dropped it just as quickly.

He didn't have to tell me what bothered him: the blood in the pictures. Randy was terrified by the sight of blood. You'd think that since his father was a surgeon, he would be sensitive to this, particularly because fainting which is caused by a strong emotion is fairly common among teenagers. It's only dangerous if the person hits their head when falling or winds up in the path of a car or something like that. In a few moments they'll wake up fine.

But Randy's dad, like too many fathers (though not mine!), believes in the parenting philosophy that forcing a child to do something which they fear will get them over it. That it might also wreck them emotionally is something which they don't consider.

I didn't tell Randy but I liked the book. Maybe I should become a doctor, I thought. We could be a good couple: me being a doctor and him a scientist. I also knew that if I became a doctor Randy would wind up as my number one patient. Like I said, some boys are high maintenance and Randy was in the top of that class too.

The first picture in the book showed hands, forceps, and the beginning of the cutting of the tissue layers of a gowned woman. Then there was a suctioning away of the amniotic fluid to give the doctor's hands more room. Finally the baby's head was lifted out, then its body, and fluid was suctioned from the baby's nose and mouth.

I found the process fascinating but Randy didn't. He began looking pale so I insisted that he lie down. I went upstairs and got him a juice box.

"Drink it all," I said, trying to imitate Erika's managerial tone. Whether it was the orange juice or feeling cared for I'm not sure, but within minutes Randy looked well enough for us to talk though I insisted that he remain lying on the couch as we did. Well, I told myself with a little smile, he had wanted to sleep over.

"Randy, we have to talk."

Now he looked nervous, like I became when I wasn't sure why my father wanted to talk to me. "OK," he said.

"Not everyone can be a doctor so that you don't want to become one like your father is completely normal. And many people don't like the sight of blood, which is OK too. But not being so afraid of it. You're a smart boy. Did you ever try to figure out why the sight of blood so freaks you out?"

"No."

"You should," I said, and changed the subject to what I really wanted to talk about, which was our relationship.

"Teenage girls bleed every month and it doesn't freak them out. Well maybe the first time it does but after that they get used to it. It's just a normal part of being a woman. Like some girls bleed when they have sex. Will you faint then? That might turn a girl off sex for life!"

What I was really asking, less bluntly, was: I am a virgin and might bleed when we first have sex. Can you deal with it?

"I know," he said. "I'll try." But with exactly what, I didn't know.

I realized that my education of Randy hadn't gone well. I had merely told him what he must already have known but I didn't know what else to say. Erika was seeing a psychologist and I'd check with her. If necessary she could pretend to have Randy's fear and leave it for her psychologist to figure out.

Chapter 40

While I don't consider it courteous to drop in on people, some cultures do. A Swedish exchange student once told me that in Sweden people just invite themselves over and this is normal behavior there. But that never was the American way so whenever I wanted to see Erika I would call her first or, if I was near the library, I would send her an E-mail.

But over the summer we had become much closer and were now more like sisters than classmates. So she told me to not bother to call: if she wasn't home she soon would be and her dad or the bodyguards would know where she was. So I could wait or check back later or ask to be driven somewhere. All their employees had been told this.

I was pleased by this change in our relationship but doubted that my family would have behaved the same. It was likely the loss of her mother and sister which had made her and her father more flexible, and her need for a real friend. Not someone seeking her father's influence but a person who valued her for herself, and this I very much was. Next to Randy, and this didn't count since he was a genius, Erika was the brightest, clearest thinking person I had ever met. I felt honored that she had invited me into her family as a sister.

This caused me to wonder exactly what she valued in me. I was honest and loyal and kept my mouth shut, but so did (some) other girls. But unlike too many of them, I also had faith in the future and believed that whatever happened, things would work out OK. Had I not survived a fatal illness four years earlier, and a murderous attack just months before? I wondered if, deep down, Erika might not have the same core of optimism about her abilities, but maybe not about her future. Could any teenager who had lost two family members be optimistic, I wondered.

Erika wasn't home when I arrived. She was keeping a therapy appointment with her psychologist. I felt that this was a good sign for I intended to ask her for advice about Randy's fear.

Though she wouldn't have minded, I didn't feel comfortable entering her bedroom without her so I sat in the hallway. Her father saw me and invited me to join him for breakfast. There was another man with him.

This man was huge. About six feet six inches tall and built like Arnold Schwarzenegger. He was blond like Abram and I noticed a faint resemblance though Abram was three inches shorter and thirty years younger. While Abram's speech was accented, this man's speech was perfect and had the English accent like you hear on the BBC news broadcasts.

The men were drinking coffee and tea. Erika's father's coffee was the usual black but the man drank his tea from a glass not a cup and he added lemon and strawberry jam to the tea like the Russian bodyguards did.

Both had nearly finished their breakfast but Erika's father insisting that I eat. The thought went through my mind that he was thinking about my family's poverty and believed that I was hungry. Though it was a kindly thought I resented such attention since my parents would sooner put their children up for adoption than let them be hungry, as some children were nowadays.

But I swallowed my pride and did love whitefish. I placed it on a whole wheat bagel and washed it down with orange juice. This was enough to satisfy him.

While I was eating, the two men spoke though what they said made little sense to me at the time. They appeared to be speaking of a serious matter and ignored me, as adults usually do when children are around. They assume that the children aren't paying attention or, if they are, that they won't understand what is being said.

"I can make your problem go away," the man said. "I can do anything you want."

"What would it take?" Erika's father asked.

"You need say only one word."

There was a silence, followed by "yes," and the man nodded.

Then Erika's father sipped his coffee and the man sipped his tea and there was another period of silence.

Erika's father asked me, distractedly, "How are your school grades?"

"I got a 4.5 average last year. Above an 'A' because of the extra credit projects I did."

He smiled. "Keep it up and I may hire you someday."

"Or perhaps I will," the man added. Both smiled but Erika's father seemed to smile more broadly at this comment and I wondered what kind of business the man had.

He was dressed like a business man, like Erika's father, but he seemed a harder person, and there was a brutal element about him though perhaps this was because of his great size. Yet I felt more protected with him than I did with Erika's father. He seemed to have a stronger, more forceful personality though I might have been wrong. One doesn't acquire billions of dollars, as Erika's father did, by being laid back.

Erika arrived a few minutes later, not looking happy. She was greeted as "princess" by the man who rose and kissed her hand. Erika's gloom instantly lifted and she grinned and threw her arms around him and kissed him on the cheek. They hugged tightly for a moment and I felt a bit jealous.

The two men left quickly and Erika joined me, nibbling on an apple tart as she drank her coffee.

"He's seems an interesting man," I said, referring to the stranger.

"Vladimir is," she replied, apparently being unsure of how much to say. Then, a moment later, she added, "He's Abram's father. He was a general in the Ninth Chief Directorate of the Russian KGB or Committee for State Security. It was that unit in the secret police which protected the highest government officials, like the praetorian guard of the Roman empire.

"He now lives in Berlin and runs a private security company. There are many of these in Europe and America. They're really private armies which sell their services to corporations and governments. America contracts with them too. He's a sweet man."

Maybe more than just "a sweet man," I thought,

as I remembered the recent conversation: "I can make your problem go away. I can do anything you want." "What would it take?" "You need say only one word." "Yes."

Had the man who so charmingly kissed Erika's hand been ordered to murder?

I wondered.

Chapter 41

Erika's gloom that morning had been caused by her therapy session. It was how she usually felt after it. When I asked why she continued therapy if it made her unhappy, she gave me a withering look, as if I was so dumb that she should have demoted me to a position fourteen steps below that of her chief assistant. It might be coming, I thought.

"When you're in therapy you experience new feelings and have new thoughts which can be scary. But I'm less depressed and happier the next day. My therapy is the most important thing in my life apart from my father."

What she said made sense though I couldn't imagine myself having a therapist. But maybe my father was my therapist, I thought, and Erika didn't have the kind of relationship with him that I had with mine. I dropped the subject.

"Speaking about therapy, I have a question about Randy."

"Let's adjourn to my room and you can lie on my couch," she said, sounding amused. Or could she be jealous, I wondered. Despite being drop-dead gorgeous or maybe partly because of it, Erika never had a boyfriend.

In her room, I went along with her suggestion and lay on the chaise lounge while she sat up on her bed. "So tell me," she said, and I did.

"Randy is a great boyfriend. He's brilliant and kind and a real gentleman. But he's also a bit crazy."

Erika laughed. "All boys are."

"Not like him," I replied, and began my explanation. "Randy's father is a surgeon." Erika quickly interrupted me. "I know. He worked on my aunt's breasts. She showed me and they've great. He's a very good doctor and very expensive. I'm keeping his card."

I was shocked. "You're perfect. Girls would die for your looks. Why would you want surgery?"

"Who can tell how I'll look once I have kids. Pregnancy changes your body."

If Randy didn't like my body after I had his kids he'd have a hard time finding a plastic surgeon who was capable of fixing him up, I thought, and continued my story.

"His father wants him to be a doctor too but Randy is afraid of the sight of blood. More than afraid, he's terrified and has fainted. He couldn't sit through one of my sister's DVDs about a shy doctor who also fainted at the sight of blood."

"So he won't be a doctor. He's so smart he can do anything and I wasn't joking about my dad maybe hiring him someday."

"His dad is also very bossy..."

"Surgeons are," Erika said, interrupting me again. This was how she usually behaved right after her therapy session. It was from being nervous, I had concluded.

"OK. But he has a big crisis now and he needs to get over it. His mother just found out that she's pregnant and they wanted another child for a long time. To be sure that Randy bonds with their new baby they're insisting that he be present at the C-section which is a very bloody business. Randy is nearly out of his mind with fear. Can you think of any way he can get rid of it? Maybe you can ask your psychologist?"

"Or say that the fear is mine and see what he says," Erika added.

"I'd thought of that too."

"OK. I'll tell you what I know though this may not help Randy. I started seeing a psychologist after my mother and sister were murdered. I began having panic attacks besides my usual depression, which you must have noticed even with my smile."

"It sounds like you were having a bad time."

"I was. Try to imagine yourself having a heart attack. First, you feel hot. Then you feel like you're going to faint and you have to get out of where you're at whether it's in class or a store. The thought goes away but it might come back the next hour or day or week. You're never sure when so you're afraid to do anything except to stay at home."

"Do you still have them?"

"No, they went away. Exactly when I can't say but one day I became sure that they were gone. That's why I say that my therapy is the most important thing in my life. I can't go back to living the life I had. It's no life.

"What Randy has is in the same class of thing that I had. They're called phobias, irrational fears, and though sounding crazy they really aren't, just like dreams aren't crazy either. Both are trying to tell the person that something about their life must change in order for them to have a better life. So the unconscious part of their mind creates this symptom in order to force this change to be made.

"Randy's fear of the sight of blood is less crippling than was mine. How often does one see blood? If his mother hadn't become pregnant he'd be fine now. But a panic attack like mine, which is just a very bad case of being nervous, can happen anytime."

"This means..." I suggested, finding her explanation to be less than clear.

"This means," Erika said, with a touch of annoyance, "that when his fear of blood arises, he must remind himself that this fear is really his friend and not his enemy, and try to figure out what change in his life it wants him to make.

"It could also be caused by a really upsetting experience relating to blood which he had when he was very young. Maybe his father did some dumb joke. Doctors don't always make the best fathers."

I then remembered that Erika's mother had been a doctor and wondered if she had been a good one. But of course I didn't say this. Agreeing with a friend that their parent is lousy is one thing but suggesting it can quickly lose you that friendship.

"I'll tell him what you said. And thanks."

It might have been the two breakfasts I had but I began feeling sleepy. So I closed my eyes and fell asleep on the chaise lounge. When I awoke, Erika was sitting up in her bed and writing in her iPad with a wireless keyboard.

She saw me move and began speaking. "I had an idea of how to get babysitters for our business."

"Welcome!"

"We make it fun, like painting the fence was made fun and not a chore in *Huck Finn*."

"How do we do that?" I asked, being unable to see how babysitting could be fun.

"Now you're being the gloomy one. OK. We start an educational group to which girls hunger to belong. The one requirement is that they babysit for us at least once a month. The group will be like an exclusive sorority."

"What kind of education would they hunger to have?"

"Read the first subject," Erika said, handing me her iPad.

I read the title, and was shocked but fascinated. Girls would kill to get into this group and I would too. The discussion was entitled: "Why You Love It When Boys Flirt With You or How Flirting Is Like Orgasm,"

"Is it true?" I asked.

"It is if my very expensive psychologist is right. Read my later notes on the page."

I did, and what she had written made good sense. I learned things about being a woman which I never realized: that my body's response to flirting was similar to what happened during orgasm but less so and in different parts of the body.

During flirting the muscles around the eyes relax and the pupils widen, while during orgasm the face and chest becomes flushed; that breathing quickens while flirting, and during orgasm there are rhythmic contractions of the uterus; and that during both flirting and orgasm there is often uncontrolled whispering.

I was hungry for more information, and burst out laughing. "You're a genius!"

"Maybe a small one," Erika modestly agreed.

Chapter 42

We sent invitations to the first meeting of the Greenwich Girls Group to fifteen of Erika's Facebook friends. Since I was the better writer, I composed it.

Dear _____,

Much information isn't gained in school. These important facts include dating skills, and which boy tries what with girls and who you should avoid.

To help you we have created the Greenwich Girls Group. There is no charge to attend our meetings but membership is open only to employees of the Greenwich Babysitting Registry LLC. Our company places babysitters in the finest, pre-selected Greenwich homes, and pays the highest rate for babysitting too.

Our first group topic is, "Flirting Your Way to Orgasm," which we are sure that you will find exciting.

We invite you to attend our group.

I signed it Erika and Margaret.

We E-mailed the invitations and waited, but not for long. Within minutes the responses arrived. All of the girls accepted our invitation. Some sent long replies stating that they had long needed such a group.

"This might be the start of another business for

us," Erika observed, noting the passion in the letters.

Our biggest problem was where the group could meet. We couldn't meet at Erika's house for security reasons: Ivan had received word that the threat from "Z" was now greater and he was checking visitors even more carefully. Adding fifteen girls to investigate would be too much.

Because of my mother's nosiness I didn't think that meeting at my house would work, and trying to get a room at the school during the summer would be impossible even with a different topic. Meeting at the local Planned Parenthood would raise unwanted questions in parents' minds. We were stumped until Erika suggested that we meet at a local day care center. Her father made a large contribution and she was sure that the center's director would cooperate. I was less certain.

"What if they ask to see our topic? 'Flirting Your Way to Orgasm' wouldn't quite cut it.'"

"Of course not," Erika replied glibly. "We have another topic. Like with companies who keep two sets of books. There is the official version, and then there is the accurate version which is kept hidden. And remember, our group is a secret sorority so the girls can't talk about what we discuss."

I was floored, and raised my estimate of Erika's value to any business by a hundred million dollars.

Despite my lingering doubts, Erika's plan worked and a week later we met in the downstairs basement room of the day care center. The girls had been advised to dress modestly and they did, for Greenwich girls that is. Many wore white knee length tennis shorts with a white shirt though one had a rose print top. The other girls wore a button-front shirt dress or stylish jeans.

Thankfully all, so far as I could tell, had worn bras. Going without a bra was a new fad at school but these were the kind of girls who hungered to discuss "Effective Habits for Success in School," which was the official version of our meeting. It was given to the day care center's director, parents, and anyone who was interested. It was as boring a topic as we could think up. To make it sound ever worse, we added some questions under it.

What kind of animal are you? Are you friendly and talkative like a chatty parrot, and do you just love doing projects for school? Or are you bold and confident like a tiger, and your friends describe you as being not afraid of anything? Or maybe you have a great sense of humor just like a monkey, and you're always joking around in school.

"It should be 'unafraid' instead of 'not afraid,'" Erika suggested.

"'Not afraid' sounds dumber," I explained, and we both smiled.

So Erika's plan worked. How could I have doubted her?

But the group's makeup surprised me. Erika had invited fifteen of her Facebook friends so I assumed that they would all be gorgeous like her and the middle school's two other stunners: Veronica and Tiffany. But these girls would, at best, be described as "attractive." They were friendly and seemed kind but none looked like the kind of girls who boys fantasize about when they are doing you know what.

When I later questioned Erika about this, she explained her choice in a few words: "'You place the beautiful girl in the front office and the hard-working Plain Jane in back.' That's one of my father's mottoes."

I shut up. Like I said, who can argue with the daughter of a a billionaire.

After passing out bottled water and juice packs (the day care center had a policy against soda) we got down business.

"How many of you have done babysitting before? It could have been with your brother or sister."

Just four hands were raised. Recent Greenwich families were into having just the one obligatory child.

Erika looked at the bright side: that we needed babysitters. But I had the feeling that these girls were thinking more about having babies. Often their glances turned from Erica to the very good looking Abram who sat watchfully in the corner. She had wanted him to wait in the car but her father's current, strict order was for him to never leave her side, and her father was the boss.

So Erika was stuck with, as she colorfully put it several times, having Abram's face stuck up her ass. Many of these girls already looked like they would have welcomed it elsewhere. Maybe Erika should buy Abram a wedding ring to wear and damn his idea about how Russian men must behave.

But Erika and I had bigger problems than that. The sex talks and dating guide to Greenwich boys would keep them involved but we'd have to educate them how to be babysitters. The reputation of the Greenwich Babysitters Registry LLC depended on that. But first things must be first and so we began with "Flirting Your Way to Orgasm or How Flirting Is Like Orgasm," a talk which wasn't all that sexy despite its title.

Basically, what Erika did was to explain how the feelings which a woman had while flirting were similar to those which she had during orgasm. She began with a question.

"How many of you girls have experienced orgasm?"

The girls looked around and some cheeks reddened. I noticed Abram staring at his shoes though I had the feeling that he was stifling a laugh. No one raised their hand though I thought that Erika might. An instructor is supposed to be more knowledgeable than their students so I expected for virginal Erika, who had yet to have her first date but was full of brilliant ideas, to begin panting and moaning on the spot. I guess that she thought better of it so she described matter-of-factly what she had learned from her psychologist, and in likely the same tone.

One fact aroused even Abram's interest: that whether a girl achieves orgasm during sex depended on the distance between her clitoris and her vagina. If the clitoris-vagina (C-V) distance is less than two-and-one-half centimeters, about the distance from the tip of your thumb to the first knuckle, the girl will tend to have orgasms reliably. If the distance is greater, orgasms will be less frequent. This research is well known and was first published nearly a hundred years ago. What to do? Erika advised the girls to experiment: "be inventive in how you have sex."

The girls began looking uncomfortable. Whether this was because it was more graphic than they expected or because of Abram's presence I wasn't sure. Erika seemed to sense this and quickly changed the topic to a more familiar one: "Boys You Should Avoid."

Here, each girl described her dating experiences and named names, while I kept detailed notes.

As I listened abstractedly, thinking whether I should measure my own C-V distance, I was jolted awake by a boy on my list: it was my Randy!

Chapter 43

"What's been your experience with Randy," the black haired girl, Naomi, asked the group, "I haven't been able to get him out of my mind since he kissed me. Maybe because I live next door to him too."

She kissed Randy, I thought, I'll murder him, I vowed. He calls me at all hours and then kisses her!

But the comments of the other girls weren't helpful. "He's real smart and he helped me in class." "I saw him staring at my butt one day." "He doesn't smile that much and I never hear him joke." "I saw him punch a boy." The last was news to me, and I wondered what else I had missed about my (former) boyfriend.

Kim raised her hand and, when Erika nodded, began speaking hesitantly. "Chris looks like Chord and that's who I was thinking of when we were together on the couch. Is it normal to be with one boy but to think of another?"

"That's as normal for a teenager as buying new sneaks but thinking about wearing another brand. At our age kids experiment; most of us won't wind up marrying the boy we're dating," assuredly replied the virgin co-leader of the group, who was yet to go on her first date. I, her virgin co-leader, nodded vigorously in agreement.

How dare we give dating and sex advice to girls as inexperienced as us, I asked myself. The only sexually active girls I knew were Laurie, who had been sleeping with her teacher, and Hillary, who had a fling with her much older cousin. For the rest of us it was just what we read about, though our books were getting more descriptive by the day.

Other girls added their comments about boys they went out with. These fell into several categories: the obnoxious ones (those who picked their nose or farted); the unfortunate ones (those with a thing about bathing or dressing properly); the creeps with continually wandering hands; and the cheap ones (plan paying for the date and forget about birthday presents costing more than a dollar). From the information gained we put together a list of twenty-three boys ranging in age from thirteen to seventeen.

"My assistant will organize your information and each girl will receive a copy at our next group meeting. What would you like to discuss then?"

I noted that my demotion to assistant seemed permanent. Our topic of flirting grabbed the girls but they suggested a more innocent tone, namely how to flirt. Doing this research would help me and Erika too, I thought, and I'd need it to find a new boyfriend. Flirting wasn't a topic in my other (Mormon) girls group.

"OK, and we'll spend the next half hour learning what you need to know to be the absolutely best babysitter," Erika added with a big smile. This topic didn't seem to grab any of the girls and I wondered how long our group would survive.

"They'll keep coming back *and* working as babysitters. Where else can they learn what they will here?" Erika advised me after the girls had left.

"About which boys pick their nose or how to quiet brats?" I asked.

"Trust me. I have other ideas."

I did trust her but I was a bit nervous too.

We split after that. Erika invited me to have lunch with her at the Terra Restaurant downtown and to then go shopping for clothes. I couldn't afford doing either and didn't like to sponge. She knew this so maybe she felt the need to be alone just as I did. My immediate plan was to confront Randy with what I had learned from Naomi.

I wasn't looking forward to it. I don't like to fight and am always afraid that my temper might get out of hand. Randy was a gentle boy but this news had pushed me to the edge. I felt like the husband who killed his wife after learning she was unfaithful. Though I knew this behavior was crazy since he could just get a new and better wife. So why did he do it? I asked myself. Because he felt that his wife was his property and that no one could steal his property even if it had been freely given. And maybe too because he had made a mistake in marrying her, so his anger was really towards—himself?

When I realized this, I became calm again, having done just what Erika's psychologist advised: to study one's feelings and not behave impulsively.

Randy and I would talk about the kiss like two adults. Then I'd slug him. I smiled as I thought this though knowing that it wouldn't happen. I had only been violent once in my life and those guys were trying to kill me.

Randy's mother greeted me with a big smile. "We'll need your babysitting business soon," she said. "Randy is in his room. He's all excited about our new addition."

He'd much rather it was a car, I thought, but I smiled back warmly. Antagonizing a future customer wasn't good business sense.

I knocked on Randy's bedroom door and walked in without waiting for a response. He was sitting up in bed and reading.

"Margaret..." he began, but I cut him off.

"Don't you Margaret me, Randy. I want to know why you kissed Naomi. And you're telling me now!"

But Randy looked puzzled, not guilty. "Kissed Naomi, the girl next door?"

"Yes, the Naomi next door. The girl who is available except when you're upset which is when you call me. How could you kiss her? I thought we were a couple."

"We are," he insisted, still looking puzzled. "I never kissed her."

"She said you did."

"Naomi said that? She's like my sister. She's lived next door since I was..." Then, as if having suddenly remembered something, he grinned at me and the thought of slugging him again went through my mind.

"I kissed her when I was five and her two brothers were holding me down."

When I heard this I felt dumb for I had done exactly what my father told me never to do: to accept a conclusion before having all of the facts. My anger, and the painful feelings it caused, were unnecessary.

I felt guilty at accusing Randy. "I'm so sorry," I said. "But this shows you how much our relationship means to me."

I sat beside him on the bed. The book he was reading wasn't his usual science or math book. Its title was another shock: *Seals In Action: Breathtaking True Adventures of the U.S. Navy's Elite Fighting Force*. Was this a new interest of Randy or had it long been there and I just never noticed. Had I pigeon-holed him as others tended to do with me ("poor" "Mormon").

"What can I do to make up for it?" I asked, now trying my husky tone for the first time.

What Randy replied, in a commanding but shaky tone, was another surprise: "Lock the door."

I nodded, and did. As I returned to the bed, I found myself wondering for the second time that day about the distance between my clitoris and my vagina.

Chapter 44

No, Randy and I didn't have sex. Neither of us had a condom and we both weren't ready.

Reading his book about Navy SEAL's may have caused Randy to think that he was, but on some level we both sensed the truth: that, being just fourteen and having grown up in our families, waiting was best for us though for how long I wasn't sure. I didn't want to wind up pregnant like Maureen had been, though that event was certainly not her fault.

What did Randy and I do? Well, a bit more than we had before, and I did wonder what his response would be if I told him the medical fact I had just learned about the clitoris-vaginal distance. And then, with great sweetness and innocence, asked him to measure it in the interest of science.

But, I didn't. As usual and like with most teenagers, my imagination sometimes runs wild.

So we lay together until his mother knocked and asked why the door was locked (all mothers must have graduated from the same school, I thought). Randy explained this by saying, using his usual naive tone, that he wasn't aware that it was. By the time he opened the door I was sitting at his computer and we both looked like kids who had been scrap-booking together or whatever.

While we easily saw through the offer of cocoa, this being another motherly trick to get us to stop what we all knew that we had been doing, we went along with it. We had gone as far as we were going to that day. But what about tomorrow, I asked myself.

The next day I felt, like they say, bummed out. The summer was only half over and I was already in danger of being murdered by "Z" and the Russian Mafia, being investigated and maybe indicted by the FBI, discovering that I might have an inadequate cervical-vaginal ratio to go along with my tiny breasts, and was still poor considering the few dollars we had made from the babysitting business and our expenses (mostly the cookies we gave away which Erika decided must now be our policy).

What else in the life of this fourteen-year-old could go wrong, you ask. Well how about Maureen winding up at my house that morning?

What happened was this. Maureen didn't like being in a hospital. Not that Rillston Hospital was a bad place for, as mental hospitals go and based on what I read, Rillston was a very good one. The food was great, the rooms were beautiful, and the staff was attentive and seemed to know what they were doing. But, despite its open door/open gate policy, it was still a hospital. No one likes being a patient and being told what to do.

Maureen had been questioned by agents from the FBI, the NSA, the CIA, and her psychologist. She had learned a nation shattering secret, interpreted for her government agent father, been kidnapped, had witnessed her parents being tortured and killed, had been raped and given birth to the child of a Russian Mafia leader, and then had her baby snatched from her while she was still nursing him. She wanted out.

Yes, she still wanted to get her baby back. Yes, she wanted to help her country. But no, she did not want to be a patient anymore.

So that morning after breakfast, dressed in her usual shorts and shirt, Maureen walked out of the hospital building onto the grounds and down the road until she came to the town's visitor's bureau. There, she looked up my address in the phone book, and called a cab.

Her arrival at my house confronted me as I lay in bed and wondered if it was worth getting up that day.

My mom spoke first. "Your friend, Maureen, is here." I opened my eyes and blinked. Had I been hospitalized at Rillston? My mother always considered me odd.

No, I was at home in my bed, looking across the room toward the beautiful face of Maureen and my mother's smile.

Maureen, being Eurasian, was obviously not a Greenwich resident. She was a newcomer and therefore must, in my mother's mind, be a potential convert to our Mormon religion. And converting a Eurasian would earn my mother many more points for the Mormon religion had an international focus. I feared that once she learned Maureen was an orphan she would be living with us. The temptation would be too great. And once our pastor's sons got a look at her they might be living with us too. Mormons take conversion seriously, you understand.

I got out of bed, put on a shirt, and acted like seeing Maureen in my room was nothing new. Not knowing what was going on, I simply said, "Hi, had breakfast yet?" I know this sounds dumb but what was I to say? Maureen, are you still crazy? Is the FBI downstairs? Has Rillston been attacked with machine guns and hand grenades? Is dad's pistol loaded? Have you called the police?

I was thinking but planning too quickly. To make

good plans requires facts and to get these from Maureen I first had to get my mother out of the room. When in doubt, try food, I thought.

"Mom, what's for breakfast?" I asked, as if I didn't know. I had been having the same breakfast (an orange, oatmeal, toast, milk, a multivitamin) for as long as I could remember.

"Downstairs, in ten minutes," she said sweetly, leaving us alone.

I took Maureen's hand and asked in the same motherly tone I used with Randy when he was going crazy. "What happened?"

"Nothing, but I can't stand being in a hospital anymore. Even my doctor said I'm not crazy, that anyone going through what I did would feel crazy at times. Otherwise it would mean that they weren't really in touch with what happened. He said that what I now need is to get back to being a normal teenager and that's what I plan to do."

"It makes sense, but why didn't you go to Erika's house. You're part of their family, not that you're not welcome here." Too welcome, I thought.

"I don't know her address and her name wasn't in the phone book. Yours was."

This also made sense. "But aren't you afraid of

what could happen to you? That you're in danger?"

"I'm not so sure. My child's father could easily have killed me but he let me go, being dropped off at the American embassy where they would be sure to take me in. To everyone except the American government, I'm just another dumb teenager. How much can a fourteen-year-old know?"

This is an attitude which every teenager understands, I thought.

"OK. But we'll have to inform Erika's father and the hospital where you are. They're probably searching for you. Then you can choose where you want to live. My parents would love to have you but though our house looks OK, we are poor. My dad is a lawyer but he's disabled with Lyme disease and hasn't worked in nearly five years. Erika's father is rich and living there you could have anything you want."

"The only thing I want is my son," Maureen replied sadly. And to this I couldn't say anything.

Chapter 45

Maureen didn't move in with us. I called Erika who told her dad who called the hospital. All decided that since Maureen was still underage she had to live with Erika and her father, who had gained legal custody of her.

Kids don't have many rights it seems though, in all honesty, Maureen would have a better life with Erika. Apart from all their money she wouldn't have to deal with my mom who, even after she learned of Maureen's move, planned to invite her to our church service. This, considering Maureen's recent experiences and worry about her son, couldn't have been high on her list of future activities.

So instead of speaking with Maureen and Erika in the Rillston Hospital cafeteria we now spoke in her bedroom in Erika's home. It had been used by Erika's sister before she was murdered but Erika and her father said it would be OK for Maureen to use it. Both felt this might help to sweep away the gloom which, understandably, still lay over the house.

Maureen saw her therapist at Rillston Hospital daily. One of the bodyguards, which now numbered twelve, drove her there. "Like with the FBI," she said casually, referring to the black color of their clothes which were either suits or slacks and a windbreaker.

My life continued along its course, with my get-togethers with Erika and Maureen being on the alternate days which I didn't spend with Hillary. All were high maintenance friends.

Since she had nothing else to do and no friends, Maureen attended our babysitting group though we never intended for her to work as a babysitter. Asking her to be with young children so soon after the loss of her son would have been cruel, apart from security considerations.

Maureen didn't really fit into the group. The members, apart from Erika, were nice but no ravishing beauties. But Maureen was a stunner and for the first minutes of the group several of the girls just stared at her, which she was probably used to. Maureen smiled back but it was not a big one, which was understandable too considering her major worry. Not how to get a boyfriend but how to get her son back. Maureen was no longer a teenager.

Both Erika and I believed that she could someday be a famous model as her mother had been, and if she wanted to. Her uncle might try to veto this choice but, as

Erika said, a girl who could survive what she did was not a girl to be bossed around. She'd probably curse him in Chinese to end their discussion.

But I'm exaggerating. While Erika's father was considered stubborn as a businessman, he was a pushover with his daughter and likely would be with Maureen too. As a parent he was a sweetheart, different from my dad but just as nice.

The topic of the second girls group was flirting. Both Erika and I felt that it was important to keep this information flowing before we began instructing them in what we really wanted them to know: how to be the best babysitter they could. We accepted that some teenagers would never make great babysitters but believed that most could be made into good ones, those who would be worth our high price without objection. During their participation in this group, though the girls didn't yet know it, we hoped to weed out who couldn't meet our standards.

Erika was some tough manager though I didn't tell her this. I still hoped to be promoted from "assistant."

My flirting lecture didn't take long. There is only so much you can say about it.

I stressed three key points: looking at the boy;

expressing interest which means getting him to talk rather than the other way around; and leaning into him with occasional touches but not you know where. Innocent ones like touching his hand or shoulder. And, of course, the importance of smiling to show that you love his company. Boys are insecure so you have to build them up before they'll risk being rejected by asking you out.

The girls looked at me like I was a genius though what I said was simply what I had picked up growing up. I checked my advice with Erika and Maureen, both of whom felt it sounded right though neither ever had a date. And, like I said, both Erika and I were still virgins and Maureen had been until she was raped.

So you might say that our group of innocents accepted advice from the innocent. But they seemed to appreciate it and probably just our talking about flirting would help all of us feel more comfortable when we actually did it.

Erika had planned for us to walk through downtown Greenwich for flirting practice but I didn't think that this would be a good idea. Having girls stop boys on the street might cause the ever-vigilant police to investigate the Greenwich Babysitting Registry LLC about other activities. You get the idea.

After I did my bit, Erika gave her first talk on babysitting: how to cope with impossible kids.

"No child is impossible," she began. "If they are it is because they are upset about something and it is your job to figure out what this is and to help them. So tell them that you feel they want something but that their having a tantrum doesn't tell you what it is. But that if they will tell you, then you will try to get them what they want.

"Now the child themselves may not know what they want, but your explanation of why they are acting as they are will give them important information about themselves so they won't feel that they are crazy. Then you can involve them in an activity or feed them or do anything else which gets them out of themselves. Are there any questions?"

Brenda asked, "What do you do if it doesn't work?"

"Sometimes nothing will work because the child is too unhappy. So accept the situation and try to engage them in something else. You're doing all that you can. The fault isn't yours."

I noticed that while Maureen had seemed distracted during my flirting lecture, she was wide awake while Erika presented her babysitting talk, which impressed me too.

After the meeting I asked her, "Where did you get all that good information?"

"I got it off the Internet of course. A good manager must be a quick study," she advised her assistant.

Chapter 46

Erika was happier on my next visit. The whole atmosphere at her house was lighter. Even the guards seemed to be telling jokes to one another though, since they spoke Russian, I couldn't understand them.

Erika's first comment to me explained everything: "'Z' is dead," to which I replied equally briefly, "Good." Then we began planning her birthday party in two weeks.

It wouldn't be a big party; just twenty invitations would be mailed. Despite her thousands of Facebook "friends" Erika had only one real friend: me. I was the only one she shared her real concerns with. Maureen's condition was still too shaky for Erika to feel comfortable revealing her problems, and Maureen had enough to worry about. She needed Erika, and Erika needed me, and her father of course.

Most of the people at the party would be the families of her father's business associates. For them, accepting the boss' invitation was a must. Also, though the threat from "Z" was now gone, every visitor to the home still had to be approved by the security group which Ivan and Abram and the other bodyguards worked for. So inviting people who had been there before and were known was easier.

Erika didn't like any of the party suggestions I made: a princess girly-girl party in which everything is pink; a fourteen-going-on-forty party in which the girls dressed older with high heels and all, based on old magazine photos; a *Twilight* party in which everything was red and black; even a nineteen-twenties murder mystery party though I had second thoughts about this.

What it came down to was that the best party for her was to give her a project and employees to boss. After that she could relax while waiting for her next project. The word "fun" didn't seem to exist in Erika's vocabulary.

But recognizing what her father wanted her to want, she chose it: my princess idea in which she dressed as a princess and the rest of us could be whatever we wanted, probably her ladies-in-waiting.

There was no real work to do. The food would be brought in by a caterer who would also clean up so everyone's job was just to have a good time.

To avoid one-upmanship, the invitation was specific: dress should be informal/casual and no presents should be brought. Instead, if desired, an anonymous contribution could be made to their favorite charity. Besides, what gift could a billionaire's daughter possibly be given that she didn't already have? As for me, my family was already my favorite charity so I felt out of the mix.

Erika's party was on a Saturday afternoon and I told my mother that I'd be sleeping over her house for a few days and would return on Tuesday afternoon. This would be the longest I had ever stayed away from home and I expected there to be a problem. Surprisingly, she agreed without argument. When I asked my older sister why this was, she related the change to the parenting class our mom had been taking at our Mormon Church.

Bless the pastor! When I heard this I asked if I could go to her Tuesday evening Bible study group at the church. I wanted to talk with the pastor: whoever made my mother less nervous deserved many thanks.

That Saturday was a beautiful sunny day with the temperature being in the mid-seventies. I wore my typical jeans and shirt which I dressed up with a red scarf, pink being Princess Erika's color. But maybe from obstinacy, I used my sister's pink Lip Out Loud Super Shiny Gloss, a freebie which she got from a magazine coupon.

When I arrived I was afraid that I would feel uncomfortable being around all the rich people and I planned to attach myself to Erika. But this proved impossible since she was the hostess and had to spread her attention. But I did find things to talk about with the teenage guests. It was mostly school stuff since we all went to the same school, or the complaints which all kids seem to have about their parents, whether they are rich or not.

Maybe because the guests were Erika's father's business associates it seemed more like a grown-up than a teenage party. There was no dancing and the music was by a classical trio (violin, harp, flute) which was soothing but certainly not rocking. The food was the expensive food which was served daily at Erika's house.

The party seemed more designed to mark an occasion than to celebrate it. But, as Erika said, "one must play their role," and she did. She exuded courtesy and good wishes and, need I say it, was even more drop-dead gorgeous than usual. I was proud to be her lady-in-waiting though she grinned when I told her this.

Finally, it was over. The guests left, the band packed up, the caterers cleaned up, and Erika and I stood looking over the water as the sun set on her dock. It was a beautiful peaceful evening.

Suddenly, a man approached us. He was dressed in the same black suit which the bodyguards wore on formal occasions. I assumed that he was one of them except that his face looked different. Though I couldn't say exactly what, I knew that something about him was wrong.

I saw him glance at Erika and, as his hand moved from his pocket, I threw myself atop Erika and we both thudded to the ground. I then felt an enormous weight upon me just before the shooting began. Blood poured over me and I lost consciousness.

Chapter 47

What I next remembered was lying on the ground and finding my clothes soaked in blood. I tried moving my arms and legs and found that they all still worked. I was blood-stained but alright.

Erika sat beside me and surrounding us were guards holding machine pistols. I could see the body of a man being dragged away and wondered if it was him that I had been suspicious of.

"He was a colleague of 'Z'," Erika later explained.

Erika was alright too. I had shoved her down and covered her with my body just before the killer began shooting. I was quicker than a guard, Grigory, who had thrown himself atop both of us and been killed by a bullet. He was unlucky. Most of the bullets were stopped by his bulletproof vest but one bullet had penetrated his neck. It was his blood from the pouring wound which had soaked us. His body lay on the ground beside us.

Not much was said that evening. Erika's father had a doctor come to the house and check us out but, like I said, we were OK.

Maureen was more greatly affected and the doctor gave her an injection to help her sleep. Such events seemed to be becoming common in her young life.

"You saved my daughter's life," Erika's father told me. "No," I replied, "Grigory saved us both."

He asked my size and said that a maid would buy me clothes to wear in place of my bloodied ones. I said that I didn't want my parents to know what happened and that these could be washed over the weekend, that I had brought other clothes for the next two days. He understood. Rich people are used to keeping secrets.

The next two days everyone just lay around. No police were called so no investigators came. The gunshots were attributed to party fireworks. Rich people value their privacy and neighbors don't question neighbors seriously in Greenwich.

Erika woke me at dawn on Tuesday morning. She told me to dress quickly and to come downstairs.

There, in the dining room, all twelve guards stood before the long table. They were dressed in black suits though I had the feeling that they would have felt more comfortable in uniforms. A ceremony was about to begin.

Erika and her father and Maureen and I stood off to a side. Ivan stood beside me and translated for us from the Russian what was being said. As he spoke, my eyes filled with tears.

First they sang the Russian national anthem.

"Russia – our holy nation, Russia – our beloved country, A mighty will, great glory – These are yours for all time!

"Be glorious, our free Fatherland, Age-old union of fraternal peoples, National wisdom given by our forebears! Be glorious, our country! We are proud of you!

"From the southern seas to the polar lands spread our forests and fields. You are unique in the world, one of a kind – Native land protected by God!

"Wide spaces for dreams and for living, Are opened for us by the coming years, our loyalty to our Fatherland gives us strength.

"Thus it was, thus it is and always will be!"

Then General Vladimir gave a speech.

"Grigory's life has lit up our spirit and our determination. Though he is dead—murdered—he would not want us to lose hope. We must be optimistic and focus on the future, cherishing each moment with those we love.

"Love is better than anger, and hope is better than despair. Remain optimistic and hopeful and we will change the world.

"To Grigory."

On the table were small golden cups holding vodka. The men raised their glasses to their lips, loudly repeated, "To Grigory," and drank it down. There was also food on the table: vegetables with boiled rice and raisins, and Russian blintzes (these are baked batter filled with cheese or jam) and the men began eating.

It was over. Grigory's body was already being flown back to the Russian town of Nikolayevsk where he was born.

Then General Vladimir spoke softly to me. "You have been stained with Grigory's blood and are now one of us. You must call me whenever you are in need. At any time, for anything," he repeated, to emphasize his point. With that, he gave me a thick, deeply embossed card. Printed on it was his name and former military rank, along with a European telephone number and E-mail address. There were two Cyrillic (that means Russian language) words printed in the corner.

"You must promise me now for I return to Berlin this morning," he insisted. I did, using the few Russian words which I had learned from the guards: "Da, da, do novyh vstrech," though I probably pronounced them wrong (they mean "Yes, yes, till we meet again.").

But Vladimir's smile told me that he had understood. He reached down, hugged me, and kissed me on both cheeks before leaving.

Erika, who had witnessed this scene, came over. "Vlad is a good man and a valuable friend," she said simply.

Early Tuesday afternoon I rode my bike home. I refused Erika's offer of a car ride. Not that I don't enjoy being chauffeured around but I felt the need to get back to my usual ordinary life, one without bodyguards and kidnapped babies.

"You're just in time. I was leaving for church," my mother said. I parked my bike and got into my father's old Malibu. It had one-hundred and fifty-six thousand miles on it but was spotless inside.

My mother started the car and turned towards me. "You have a small cut on your chin," she said. I looked in the rear view mirror. She was right. I touched the beaded necklace which Mother Marie had given to me. It had been blessed by the Orisha Gods to insure my normal life span. One of the beads had been shattered when a bullet glanced off it, this causing the bullet to miss its mark and for my life to be saved. It was a fragment from this bead which caused the scratch on my chin.

Was this an accident or a sign that Babaluaiye, my God husband, still approved of me. I didn't know.

Perhaps Mother Marie would know or maybe not.

I remembered the Chinese proverb which Maureen had spoken to the spy: *man proposes and God disposes.*

"It's a prayer meeting," my mother said, "I hope you're not bored." Her parenting class certainly was changing her, I thought. In the past she never would have made that remark.

"No, mom, I won't be bored. In fact, I'm looking forward to it."

Now it was my mother's time to be surprised. "Are you well? You look tired."

"Yes, I'm tired. It was a busy weekend."

I closed my eyes but, though feeling worn out, I still had things to do when I got home. I hadn't spoken with Randy all weekend and knew that he must need me. A woman's work is never done, I thought, as I tried to doze in the few minutes before we reached the church.

I prayed that afternoon for all of us: for me and Erika and Randy and Maureen, for my family and their families, and for Maureen's baby, who lived *somewhere* far across the Pacific and cried for his mother.

It was seven when my mother dropped me off at Randy's house. He seemed where I had last left him, sitting up in bed and reading his book about Navy SEALs. I told him what had happened and he was shocked but not surprised. Nothing about what I involved myself in had the power to shock him anymore.

But something had puzzled me since the day Grigory was killed.

"How did I know that man was a killer?" I asked Randy. "I'm sure that I never saw him before."

Randy smiled. "Not his face, but his facial muscles. People can read facial muscles and interpret their underlying emotions. I'm not good at it but apparently you are very talented. There's a psychologist in California who trains FBI and CIA people so they become able to read faces better though probably few are a natural like you or ever get as good. You're a rare girl."

Now I didn't mind that he had smiled and I smiled back. "Of course I am, I chose you for my boyfriend."

Boys like to think that they are the ones who do the choosing so I didn't know how well my line would go over. Also because, like many hasty remarks, it hadn't gone quite right and made it seem as if I was saying that no other girl would want him. But Randy didn't appear to notice. He tossed his Navy SEALS book onto the floor and looked towards me.

"Lock the door," he ordered in his still shaky but commanding voice.

I gave him a long look.

Then I walked toward the door and obeyed.

www.ingramcontent.com/pod-product-compliance
Lightning Source LLC
Chambersburg PA
CBHW030909120626
46554CB00001B/76